THEY BUILT A GALLOWS FOR YOU AND ME

CODY W HIGGINS

DEATH'S HEAD PRESS

an imprint of Dead Sky Publishing, LLC
Miami Beach, Florida
www.deadskypublishing.com

ISBN: 9781639510184

Cover Art: Justin T. Coons

The "Splatter Western" logo designed
by K. Trap Jones

Book Layout: Lori Michelle
www.TheAuthorsAlley.com

This
story
is,
lovingly
dedicated
to
my
Sarah
Darling.
Without her it could not be.

INTRODUCTION

DUST SWARMED AND created a veil between the two lovers. Encapsulated in a separate universe from all the rest, yet unable to see. Eyes crusted oceans. He reached up, to brush the dirt from her face. Thinking of her. First. Still. Hand hesitant in the air, confused by old habits in movement. Needing to retrain its most base reactions. He didn't think he'd be able to. And she knew he wouldn't. Which is what led them here in the first place.

Emptiness. For miles and miles. A sore, bitter emptiness but for the dirt that wind kicked up into the air, and the looming gallows that stood proudly in the desert. She could taste his tears, held deep behind lying eyes, 'You don't have to. We can just go.' Hair bouncing as her head shook from side to side. 'People die all the time.' He flinched. Muscles tightening. Eyebrows quivering, telling the entire story of his life to those in tune enough to read it. 'I can't see you,' wind calming on cue, sand falling gently on shoulders, in hair, finding home back on the ground, 'through all this.'

'That's why we're here,' he mumbled, knuckles halfheartedly rapping against the clean, bright smelling wood of the gallows.

1

'It's hard to hear you when . . . '

'YEAH IT'S FUCKING HARD TO HEAR ME ISN'T IT!?' Skin painted red from the inside out, 'That's why we're here,' as he slumped against trees torn down and manufactured into splinters of what they once were. Splinters broken off and inched into skin as his body slid down to sit on steps.

She clenched her jaw. Not sure why. Wishing he would, like he used to. Teeth held tight together, hands rubbing at thighs, something, anything to be familiar again. Anything to see him hurting again. Knowing her fingertips on his warm skin would sooth him. All those nights filled with razor blades hungrily eating through soft flesh. Blood drip drip dripping onto tiled floors like faucets with blown O-rings before it teased enough and came running down, hot red tears from tears, and splattered the floor. She knew how to clean that mess up. Warm soapy water. Rags squishing out bubbles as they were rung out. This. This was something different. Something rags and stitches and time were not going to fix.

'Nothing's going to fix it. Except a tight rope and a quick drop.' Words casually breaking the silence.

'I can take the baby and go. I'm sorry. You can start fresh.' He could smell the pleading in her words. Stung his nose like the first breath after walking into a house stained with cat piss.

'I didn't want to start fresh,' voice skipping in the air, 'I wanted you . . . I wanted . . . ' His body moved automatically. An automaton inside living skin. Turning to step. One after another, after another, up the steps to the platform waiting patiently for their drama to unfold. The platform didn't care. Only there to serve its purpose, grinding underneath heavy footsteps. The heaviest anyone had ever seen. Though there was something different about theseones. Not as heavy. Not as full of longing for another day, another hour, another second.

Eyes scanned the barren canvas as he reached the top. Cold hands reaching for tightly wound rope. Cold, even though the air around was hot and dry, shimmering in the constant sunlight. Seemed the sun never set in this place. And as he slowly pulled the noose round his anxious neck, something changed in the landscape. Figures rose out of the dirt. Crumbling bits here and there, as we all do in life. Crashing to the ground, clumps of dirt exploding with loud bursts like birds blown apart with firecrackers.

The dirt-figure audience stood behind her as she watched on with blurred vision. What could she do but watch his performance now? Listen for the break of his bones? Smell his soul as it spilled from his lifeless body and burned away in this god forsaken desert? Not much. She feared she'd faint in the heat. Knees locked straight like nervous teens giving reports in the front of the class. Breathing, heavy and patterned with sadness. She whispered through closed lips, 'I love you,' like she used to. So long ago when he could still see her thoughts in her eyes. But now . . . now he didn't notice.

He stepped over the hole covered by hidden trap door, and quickly pulled the lever before he had time to look at her, knowing he'd falter if sight had even a moment for doubt. Though as the door fell open, and feet cascaded towards ground, world twisting in slow motion, he locked eyes with her, her love and his regret, wishing things had ended differently. And suddenly, violently, he slammed into the ground.

Rope snapped screaming old apologies for its failure. Neck pulled up from body but no worse than casual whiplash in collision. Dirt pretending at executioner audience fell apart and blew into the wind. They never stick around. But she was still there. Covered in dirt. He breathed in deeply, mouthfuls of ground, sky, sun. He could taste her through the dry earth, a gentle breeze through summer picnic memories. And she sobbed. A loud, ugly sob, geese dying in backyard cages with no more water allowed.

They both coughed. Hands reaching to throat as though twins separated by hundreds of miles who still somehow mimicked each other's actions. She wanted to rush over to him. To tell him, in so many pleased-with-themselves words, that this was providence. It was surely a sign that God, or the universe, or *whatever* wanted him to live through this space. But she didn't. She knew he already heard the whispers in the hot desert heat. Already had a plan to get through it. A plan that involved razor blades, and shadows, and stitching darkness into blood. A plan to give them the hanging, they so desperately cried for.

CHAPTER 1
HOMECOMING

THE SAND WAS hot in the high sky. All the way up through each of the layers. If there were, in fact layers of sky to the sky; Jezebel thought as she watched the heat of the sand shimmering in air like magic from Papa's finger tips, walking some odd feet off behind Papa, just outside the town that he and Ma told her would be home for the next bit of time. Always was a bit of time, asking Papa, never the whole time.

'Pa, is there layers to the sky?' Jezebel's voice danced out in the heat like rain drops on leaves.

Her Pa stopped walking. Wiping the sweat simultaneously off his brow as he looked upwards into the sky, 'Reckon there's layers to everything,' turning to wink at her, 'don't you think so?'

'I don't know, I guess so.'

James rest gently in the carrier Ma had made special for the trip, slung naturally across her front. Ma said she learned it from watching the savages when she was younger. Always making it sound like her time there, with them, was only some sort of casual visit. Like the ones Francis and I used to spend with Grandpa before he died. Grandpa's death being about 3 years ago now, I reckon. Pa said his heart gave out. But Pa doesn't know. The wolves got to his body long before anyone else. Maybe was the *wolves* that killed him. Whether teeth in bone or eyes in window. Was the threat of death all we needed to die? Was it all about when and where we broke down, sore, beaten, too tired to fend the wolves off into the shadows yet again? Reckon it was his heart gave out after all.

Francis would remember those times with Grandpa, for now. Though they would likely fade for her with time until hollow like husks of memories. James would never even have those husks. His leftovers of time being only the leftovers of other peoples' stories about Grandpa.

Assuming we all lived long enough to tell stories of Grandpa to a James old enough to listen. Was why rivers spoke so little, and in such hushed tones. Hushed for fear of sounding younger than one was. Hushed for fear of not listening. And remembering even through the stories of others' experiences.

'Jezebel, honey,' Pa breaking her train of thought with his tone, dry and heavy, more scratch than not, from the dust of the trail, 'I want you to stay close now, you hear? Gettin' close to town. Always more eyes at the entrances. And hurry your sister up.'

Francis was five. She'd turned five last August. Ma and me made her a pie. It was so good that I sort of hoped she didn't like it much; more for me. Papa would only have one piece. Maybe same for Ma. James would only have bites. Always the smallest of things. Except love and crying, it seemed.

'Bel!' Papa hollered from even further up now. 'Your sister.' Eyes instructing direction.

Feet slowed. Jezebel had to get further from Papa, Ma and James in order to 'hurry up' her sister. A point she didn't bother sharing with Pa. 'Francis you need to hurry up. Pa wants us to stay close coming into town. You know how folks can be.'

The little girl kicked at pebbles only youth could see with bare feet as she scampered along, shoes in one hand, a dead dandelion bouquet in her other, at a speed that looked hurried but wasn't.

Jezebel laughed.

'What are you laughing at?' Her sister pondered.

'Nothing, Francis. Will you hurry please? Papa is gonna get angry if we lag too far behind.' Francis dropped her eyes at this. Her bottom lip curling over. Face sad before emotions. Jezebel wondered if how we felt didn't just mimic our face all the time. We become what we present. 'What's a matter?' As she ushered her on.

'This isn't gonna be like last time is it? I told Papa I didn't want to go. He didn't listen.'

'We had to leave,' all weight left in her voice for the last words, 'you know that.' The little girl said nothing, and only ran off through a cascade of dust and dirt both created and creating as she hurried to catch up with her parents.

We linger till we don't. We hurry till we can't. A perseverance that even twelve-year olds, even five-year-olds, could connect to, could see and feel in themselves and others. Maybe even baby James, as well. Maybe it was in our marrow. Maybe it was the consciousness that led us through this world. A simple acknowledgment of perseverance. Maybe made consciousness feel like persecution. Or persecution feel like consciousness. Where so many babies wouldn't survive the trail, James had, and maybe that was proof enough of the perseverance of his tiny will. Though just because he was small, Jezebel thought, didn't mean his will was.

Jezebel didn't hurry as Francis had. Walking, not slowly, but not quickly either, following the footsteps of her family (mostly of Francis as her hurry had covered up so much else of the travels ahead of them, even of Jezebel's footsteps both towards and away from the direction of their new home) along as the trail became less and less dusted.

The sparse landscape had, too, become more populated the closer they got to the town. Trees finding reason and condition to push up through what was, mostly, dry and endless field. Jezebel could at one point, for what must have been miles and miles, count the trees she saw on two hands, maybe half a foot as well. She giggled now, thinking of her having half a foot. Though it was cut short when she thought of how difficult their travel would have been had she had half a foot on one side.

Thank God for the way things worked out. All happening as it must. She, too, having happened as she must.

Trees seemed to blanket the earth more and more, getting evermore denser, as they walked on, Jezebel slowly catching back up to the group.

Pa had said the town was called Salina. And that they suffered greatly in the war. He told us they'd likely be leery of strange travelers. Seemed everyone was leery anymore. Always was? The way we were made? Made to be leery. Made to be weary. Made to be.

Jezebel didn't care much what the town was called. Everything needing to be called all the time. Needing definition and terms for its shape. Terms for the town meant terms for her. And that bothered something in her. Though, she thought, it was nice it started with an S, at least. Letting that carry her on further into its heart.

They'd all been worn down during the travels. Well maybe all 'cept James. He stirred a bit at this. Broadening a smile on Jezebel's face. As if to contend with her assessment of things. Something wanting to contend with our assessment all the time. The great human strain; living through the contention of time. Living through time contended by all things with which the universe was capable of sway; James, dirt on trail, grass in wind.

She had been here before. Each of them had. Each of us *has*. All known. All felt deep in our bones. Her footsteps not only falling in the wake of her Pa's, or Ma's, nor even Francis's; but in all steps, those who've come, and those yet to. It was sad to forget our steps. Though maybe necessary. Maybe we'd never take another, if only we could remember.

Eyes glinted out from some of the houses, broken souls in broken windows selling broken stories that nobody believed in anymore. We are only a fairy tale, thought Jezebel, a fiction, and not only that, but one that's entirely unbelievable. She wanted to be real. Wanted to mean something more than just what people said. Wanted the eyes watching them, searching her, to be something different than before; something more than the same story time and again. This time would be different, Pa said. This time.

A bright looking fellow came strolling out from what looked like the General Store, some 500 or so feet ahead of where the family stood in forward motion. His face had seen more than its fair share of dust. Though a handsome look. An untrusted kindness came along with that charm. A certain persuasion.

'Hello there!' His voice was handsome too. Confident like the calls of wild animals. But something taunting in it as well. Something smirking.

'Hello back.' Papa was reserved, though playing the game, Jezebel heard in the nuances falling from his tone.

The man came closer now.

We stopped walking.

'Why hello!' His big grin scanning us like monsters in the dark playing friendly. I could taste it sweating off him in the heat and rolling out over all things close enough. Like oozing masquerade. 'I'm Jebediah, welcome to Salina!' he raised his hands out next to him in mock display, pausing awkwardly, 'what brings y'all through this way?'

'Lookin' for the Zeen place.'

A silence as words were given place to die; as motives were given place to kill. 'Bo Zeen?'

'That'd be the one.' A tone in Pa's voice that made Francis step over and behind him to Jezebel, squeezing her hand as she did.

'Bo died not long back.' Jebediah spit to the side in a defining way. As though it somehow drove the point further. Steer whipped into service. Man whipped the same.

'I know that,' offered Pa, 'I bought the house from his sister, Matilda.'

'Matilda you say?'

'Yes sir.'

'Ain't nobody seen or heard from Matilda in some time,' his eyes continuing to search along with his words. Pin pricks looking for air.

'All the same. Think you could point me in the right direction?' Pa holding still.

Jebediah pointed us onward. He told us it was a pleasure having fresh faces around. And his words almost believed him. Said once the family got settled in, he'd love to introduce us around. Ma said that'd be just fine. Pa only watched the man with a half grin on his face, the other half hidden in sunlight. Jebediah was a man who lived in the shadow of the wind, Pa would say later. Wanting to be real so bad (the trailings of dust), he'd force other folks' will. Wasn't a man to be trusted, but easily enough placated.

Placated like water in river. A shifting ease.

The house was only a few years old. Wood still seemed freshly cut. A house young enough didn't yet seem it had even taken its first breath. Though cut the same. Cut into existence. Too many not being able to see that all existence was shape, was cut out of nothingness.

It would have talked if it could. Pa said. Well, not exactly but similar before even getting there. Said it was building this house what killed Bo Zeen. Sometimes making home takes more out of a man than he has to give. But sometimes ya ain't makin' a home for yourself; no, instead makin' a home for someone else. Pa told the girls that this home had been made just for them, with a quiet sparkle in his eye, but, he warned, don't tell the others.

'Why not Pa?'

He smiled that rare smile, 'Folks don't always respond well to destiny, darlin', find it don't sit well in many stomachs.'

'But I hear people say "everything happens for a reason" all the time.'

'But what they mean, Bel, is everything happens for *their* reason.'

Jezebel thought of her father's words as they approached their new home, it whispering out hellos as they neared close enough to hear. All a measurement of close enough to hear. Though that doesn't appear to have much bearing at all on understanding what it is that we *do* hear. Some things sink into a pond. Other things float to the other shore. Humanity caught in both. A tightrope like walls between the understanding of self through things we embrace, as well as through the things we lose. Eventually it all turns to loss anyway.

Be thy curse.

The house spoke to Jezebel that night, as she knew it would. Pa had said to her once, while night gave way to day, in that early morning but still feeling darkness of night space, her young mind up and reeling from nightmares, or downmares; that houses didn't get lonely. How could he be so sure though? Ma had never been so sure of such things. Though, thinking on it, Jezebel couldn't think of her mother being much for certainty about anything at all. Or, not much at all, at least.

But Bel heard the loneliness in the voice of wall and floor, ceiling and window, in the moments where the rest of the world quieted down enough to be able to make it out. Always loneliness in the voice. And this house was no different.

'We hear what we wanna hear,' Pa had told her that night, as well as many others, 'if you search in the world, or anywhere else, for that matter, for somethin' in particular . . . you're bound to find plenty of it, darlin'.' She liked when he'd call her darlin'. Made her feel grown up, made her feel as beautiful as Mama. But she knew, also, there was somethin' in what Pa meant when he said it, somethin' she didn't quite understand. And that didn't make her feel grown up. That didn't make her feel as beautiful as Mama. It made her feel like a lonely little girl; as lonely as houses that no one would listen to.

So, she sat on a spot on the floor, not just in the corner but close enough to, to be somewhere that likely hadn't ever gotten much attention. And she quietly listened to the lonely song.

Splinters in skin;
it begins,
but doesn't last like fast
forwards of flowing flower flutters,
growing garden gutters,
and ripping up floorboards, one's own skin,
    in attempts to not
feel again.
Splinters, take hold
in old
    familiar ways,
bleeding breaths bubbling through

lungs drowning in attacks
filled with the panic we
thought windows could fight back,
    but learn . . .
We're suffocating with each breath,
we're living for each death,
we're bleeding to be the best,
we're, alone like all the rest,
like all the rest,
    till she steps
    into us,
    and I becomes we.
    You becomes me.
    Splinters become,
    home, & bone, & . . .
        not so alone.
Not so,
        darkened in the night,
    wisps of wind carrying dust,
    kicking rain into your
    eyes, like love from
        surprise
            strangers
        joining you for
    the night.
Splinters kill the loneliness,
being bits of life we
regress into parts of ourselves
most never bother to spend
time in.
    But the ones who
    do, are magical.
The house thinks I'm magical, Bel, thought, late

that first night, in a new town, in a new home, with new dirt, and new sown-stitches holding skin to bone, holding it to her own, cries lost to silent winds pretending at chimes to give signs of things yet to come, stories left undone.

And as Bel got to know the floorboards of their new home; Francis dreamed dreams she couldn't tell.

The travel to their new home had been hard on Francis in ways she wouldn't be able to understand till much later in life, if life so chose to carry her journey that far. Life making the decisions for us in those dark spaces where we are afraid even, maybe most of all, to look at the light. Afraid for what it may shine upon the things we couldn't see before. Out of sight out of mind. And maybe that was it; our mind left out in the void of life when we least expect it.

There had been something in the way the world turned beneath their, or, least beneath *her*, feet as they walked from used-to-be-home to soon-to-be-home. Some lives lived forever in that space. Francis hoped hers wouldn't. Francis hoped this new home, this soon-to-be-home would be different than last time. She couldn't say how or why, (Ma and Pa hadn't taught her the words yet) but there was something sickening in what they left behind as they moved on. Maybe that was all of us. Maybe evolution itself left something sick, behind; maybe the path of our change itself was sickening, was somehow vile and rotten.

That was why the journey had tasted so bad in her young, little bones. That was why her dream was the same for so long. Sticky and sour in her mouth. Consciousness sick in the moment between selves.

A heavy orange tint hung deep in the sky above

their home. Always the exact same tint, the exact same hue, but yet, somehow not. Mind tracking change, mind tracking the times it had been here, in this same moment, and *knowing* it was different though the same. The moon, full, held itself like hanging horse thief outlined somewhere behind the orange cloud coverage so thick in the sky as to be an all-encompassing atmosphere. This was all of existence; Francis just knew it.

Knew it in the way wind blew through her hair, ruffled under her skin, with that same orange tint that surrounded her. We become our atmosphere, even if it's truly someone else's. Our atmosphere being not our own making for so long. Some never knowing one of their own.

It was how Francis felt; that this wasn't her own atmosphere. But she would learn in time to come that it was, is, would be, more her own than she could have imagined. Time standing still here though, watching, like so much else, to see what would happen.

Her feet felt familiarly bare in gravel steps as she hesitantly shuffled towards the house set against the background like earth set against the background of darkened space. A home being all. Francis wore shoes as little as possible. And so her soles were used to the way she wore indents of stones. She hardly even noticed it. Ears picking up the light grind of rock against rock as she stepped forward, more than feeling each step in the nearly suffocating silence floating around the scene. Felt like a scene. How life felt after you lived it. Memory a moving picture book of moments that no longer feel as real as we have to believe they were, want to believe they were, or are.

Cause if our memories weren't real? What reality was there in the moments we build the memories from? A proposition too difficult to treat with any sense of seriousness. This was real, Francis had told herself, which was precisely why the steps felt so familiar. What could be more familiar than real?

The door opened on its own as the little girl hovered to the threshold. A greeting home after so long away. But, where had she been, it asked her.

She could not answer.

She did not know.

The only truth in where we have been when we have been away from home was a lie. Never honest. Always made up. Made up in that way that wants to be, needs to be, believed for its very own falsity. When we play pretend, little hands on little handles in little homes lit with little candles, we are truth in our own skin. But as soon as we say the reasons why;

Why did it take so long?

Where have you been?

Who were you talking to?

we become lie. We become reason and excuse and explanation.

'Never,' she could remember as the door subtly closed behind her, Pa saying once, 'never explain yourself, Francis. It can only ever be a lie.' Pa felt, there was nothing worse you could do to someone than lie to them. Rather, he would say, a knife be plunged deep into his chest, eyes met against his own, than be told an untruth. At least there was dignity in violence. Or could be.

Something felt like a lie here, as that same hue had followed Francis into the walls of her home.

Something felt like lie, like an excuse for being away. No windows to let in light. Yet that glow infected sight. Maybe that was it, she thought, maybe it wasn't her surroundings at all but instead the tint came from her own eyes. The lies we are told really only being in how we see.

And finally she saw.
And finally the sight same,
down the stairs,
like sauntered sex
selling soothing, so
sensual sleuths slyly
surveying sinners wouldn't
catch.
Caught,
like buy me
a lie & I'll
testify that
life
was good
at the end of
the trip
when only God
is left
paying
attention.
But even God
didn't pay
attention
enough.
Enough.

And the house whispered to her. Enough. And she followed the tint up the stairs; sight leading body.

Action always following sight. even if sight is blind and only pretense of perversion pooling in pores of poor blind girls who'd wandered too far from home; wandered too far and only had lies as reasons why. Because die, was at the end of the tunnel. Die, was at the top of the stairs, waiting like always. Always being that forever we toss around so easily.

The room opened up at the top of the stairs, unlike how it felt in real life. But that didn't matter here, not in the moment. Never in the moment. In the moment all we have is the lie how we see the world. No thought, but only response. And even later, in hindsight, all we had to think of was response tainted by tint in sight as memories of reality to decide and judge our own existence by, with.

Was this real?, Francis thought inside a dream. But of course it was real! Of course even the suggestion of the question *of* was kin to blasphemy. For our sight was vision of the world, vision of God, and what could be more real than that?

Someone cried off in the distance. Hue the same, but, darker, quieter, here. Sight having that much more reason to question itself. She cried in that soft whimpering way that suggested it had been such a very long time since her eyes, her cheeks hanging and tired on her face, had been dry. A whimper that had more sadness at sadness in its melody than sadness plain and simple. Though maybe that was *all* sadness, whimpering melody or otherwise.

Francis watched her, listened to her, in the quite orange hue hesitantly as she undreamingly took sad steps closer and closer. Sad because she'd been here before. Sad because she'd seen how this played, how

CODY W. HIGGINS

this ended, even if she didn't know it. We all know how it plays out. Sure, we act like we don't. We seek counsel. Whether God or any other idols. But in our souls, we know. Like a song played that we hear the melody before it finishes its last note, last breath. Francis felt the melody of this little dying girl's last breath deep inside her. Unshakeable. As if our new evolution. Changes in moments that aren't fully understood but will be lasting in us forever.

'Hello?' Francis's little voice sounded that much smaller against the gravity of the scene she walked into. The weight of the world we were in, playing such a role in what we *are* in it.

'Closer,' something, someone, whispered far off in the misty black shadows that shaded this orange hued atmosphere as drawings done by amateurs. Something slightly unbelievable about it. A thing taunted her mind to believe this was it, this was the reality to end all other things. It wasn't the girl, since her crying didn't cease. 'Closer . . . ' and again. And Francis, though tumbling into terrified tension; couldn't help but to step forward, step onward towards the crying girl, towards, the taunting shadows.

'Why are you crying?'

Her words burst into a red mist that came back down from air already full to cover the ground, cover the girl, cover herself in a damply dry layer of burning red blood. The girl's cries turned to screams as the mist hungrily helped itself to her sweaty skin, slipping and sliding into gaps made by imagined teeth tugging tenaciously at its frayed fabric; reality in the covering of things.

Tears of fear and sympathy of instinct began to roll down Francis's face building in ocean-sized puddles at her feet. And in a moment before looking down at the burning, red gaps in her flesh, she could see the whisper step out of the shadows, a shadowed whisperer that looked, that looked . . . exactly like Ma. Eyes met down, hard to pull from the familiar creature yet not, stepping both from and into familiar setting yet not, but tingling was too great to ignore, and as her eyes saw, lips burst forward. Francis couldn't hold back fear any longer. As the red mist of her own inquiry into of the world ate away at her young, delicate skin. Flesh disappeared into hunger, as Francis began screaming a scream that overshadowed everything else happening. All things; crying girl; bleeding hungry mist; whispering whispered mothers; familiar hue and home alike; all retreated to the nothingness that came before existence at the overwhelming tones of the screams that roared from Francis in a stream of the creation and destruction of all things. Birth and flood, condemnation and redemption; all in the single moment of unrestrained fear that came from a little girl watching her skin whispered away under flame, of dreams more real than fantasies themselves would ever want to admit. Real like fantasies we'd *never* want to admit.

Ma woke first. To Francis's horrified screams spilling like smoke around fire from her little sleeping body. She hadn't known her little girl was still sleeping though. Who could be?

'Honey,' she spoke into darkness filled so up there was room for nothing else. But maybe . . . maybe nothing was ever so full as that. Maybe there was always room for just a bit more. Though, if we are always capable of just a bit more, we are always capable of all a bit more. The darkness wasn't too full of Francis's screams for Ma's words as she stood up out of bed, 'Honey it's only a dream, you're okay,' but only she hadn't spoken loud enough to make notice. Speak loud enough to be noticed. Or listen to the screams around her.

As she sat on the bed beside, Ma could tell Francis was still asleep. She gently placed a hand on her shoulder, and eyes crying sprung open while the screams died in quiet but suffocated breaths, becoming in sobs.

'You're burning my skin! You're burning my skin!' Francis yelled at intended soothing touch from her mother. Pa and Jezebel awake now too, sleepily startled into some odd type of chaos. Our settings sometimes change. But the dreams will follow. This was home. And there was a mist in the sky.

CHAPTER 2
THERE'S BLOOD IN THE WATER

THE NEXT FEW DAYS brought about regular life. Life did that more often than not; oscillated into some 'days go by' type of routine: whether new home, new skin; or more of the same: then, occasionally, slipping back into some unavoidable chaos. Jezebel was old enough to know what the slipping felt like, what it was. All it takes, all it ever takes, is the one step. One step at a time. Francis was too little to know such things, Jezebel thought. And certainly James. Probably her friend Nancy as well.

Nancy was a straw-haired girl, a few years younger than Jezebel, that Bel had met the day after their first night. Her father, Jebediah, owned the General Store nearest them. She looked like the daughter of a man like Jebediah, of a man *called* Jebediah, to Bel. Was interesting how that worked. How we could look like what we're called, or who's called around us. It was a truth in any case. If our skin didn't tell who we are, if our names didn't tell who we are, then what good was having either? Made Bel wonder if she did, in truth, look like a Bel, look like the daughter of her pa. She looked intently at Nancy, wondering this fairly unrelated thought, half expecting Nancy to inquire at her. Nancy only smiled timidly at the older girl.

She was happy to be out of the house, out of the shop, and off on adventures with new friends. Jezebel had an air about her that Nancy had never sensed from anyone else in her short years. Something, in a way, that felt older not only than herself, but than even the adults she'd been around. A certain quiet certainty that could only possibly speak on its own account if it had been around a long, long time. Nancy felt Bel could get her to do anything, cause there was wisps of 'everything is okay' flailing about her like a tail of dust drifting behind tired buggy. A pulling gravitas. But in the same breath: there was nothing, it felt, that Bel would pursue that could possibly be bad; so no real reason to object in the first place. We so often want to give in to those gravitas people who step into our lives. We want to lose control. But we need those gravitas people to let us know we'll still be safe . . . ish. Giving self over to the other in this way can be exciting, liberating, and intoxicating. It can also tear us apart. Sitting in the heavy dark, eating strips of our skin left dangling on our sacrificed frame, expression still of surprised abandonment of tragedy. So when Bel told Nancy there was a pond she saw some several miles south of town, outside the prairie grass and into the stretch of woods there; Nancy felt it must be safe to explore.

Though still some hesitation.

'Are you sure there's a pond there?'

'Pond . . . Nancy . . . It's practically an ocean. You've never seen it?'

'I've never been that far out of town. Certainly,' her voice trembles even in the safety of her brave friend, 'not out to the tree line.'

The tree line. Mind as tree line. Humanity as tree line. Confines that allow us to understand, allow us to be understood. All like tree lines off in the distance that we've always been told to stay back from. Scared, maybe most of all, by our own desire to see what's being kept back beyond its border.

'You're not scared of the woods, are you?' Bel taunted.

Nancy kicked at stones in grass below her feet, 'Mother says it's not natural for 'em to be there.'

Jezebel giggles, 'Your mother thinks it's not natural for trees to be in the woods?'

'Not just,' Nancy stumbles over words she doesn't fully understand such fear of, 'she says the woods shouldn't be there. It's a great big circle in otherwise clear prairie for miles and miles . . . seems, off, I reckon.'

They walked on in quiet for a bit but for the sound of their feet on the ground. Maybe the most human of sounds. Evolution walking away. Made it hard for those left behind. To listen to our songs.

'Your mother is just scared of herself, you know? That's what Ma says. Folks make all these boundaries for themselves cause they're too scared of who they are. So we all box ourselves up and make up these stories about unnatural woods and scary fairytales to blame it on.' Neither girl said much again for a spell. Each weighing desire is all any people are ever doing; weighing desire against desire and picking a path. Picking what will, hopefully, satisfy us the most. 'And besides . . . you've never even been out of town, your mother probably hasn't either.' Jezebel smiled at Nancy, 'But I have. And I can tell you, it's an ocean worth seeing, Nancy, and . . . perfectly safe.'

Feet moved on as Nancy nodded and smiled back at her convincing friend. A simple ease existed between the girls as though they had been friends for years and years and this was another adventure on a long, long list.

There was something, in the grass, lifted off and carried away by the wind, that, wasn't a warning to the young girls, but instead a notice, of things to come. Or at least an attempt at such things. It knew the scene ahead, and in fact more than that, more than told, more than listened for. The wind had lived through these stories told. We could smell it in its particles, but could never say. Memories of memories we aren't allowed access to. Tell me of history and I'll tell you of lie.

The girls could smell it. But they couldn't say. And only walked on, further, towards the edge of the woods.

'They look beautiful.' Nancy spoke nearly in awe as they stood just outside the forests diameter. As though another world. And in that instant, in that moment, there was something more in our boundaries than what Bel's ma had said, something in how our worlds swam amongst each other. Because there was definitely some distinction between the world of these woods and the world surrounding; and probably the worlds surrounding that, ad infinitum. Always a thing, a new, to step into. So often that thing being one another. Step into me and I'll step into you.

And, of course, the world is never the same after. It was never the same to begin.

Always a fair trade though. Bel could feel the trade as the girls stepped foot over boundary and into the woods. A simple longing lingered lustfully from the prairie they left behind. It played quietly. But would have been tragically loud if only it had had the ability to be so. All of our once-upon-a-times functioned in that way. Some were just better at wielding razor blades than others: cutting into us so we won't forget where we've been, so we can't see where we're going.

'Are you sure there's an ocean in here?' Nancy held off decision while Jezebel answered, but she couldn't hardly believe there was any water in this place, let alone an ocean-sized bit. Something in these boundaries whispered in her little ear, though. It said wet things in a language she didn't understand. Answering the questions before Bel could. Many before Nancy could even ask. Head reeling with the chaos of calmed coercion convincing connivers that it was their idea all along. Which was good. Good because Jezebel had her own chaos to deal with. Fantasies sung in dead bird song for too tight wires in a cage.

It was like,
I used to remember,
if you'd only tell me why.
It was like,
the cold winds
of November,
in the middle of July.
It was like,
why?

Why me?
Why flee from fighting
figments of ghosts &
goblins & witches
with magic in fingertips?
It was like,
poison on lips,
and children with
hits defining
future.
Future for trees
watching us lose ourselves.
Future for fear of
the way death smells.
Bel could, taste that smell,
deep in forest's breath.
Future for,
how it felt with nothing left.
Nothing left but
cold backs
turned to
cold stone
in
oceans in forests,
waiting all alone,
all alone for little
girls try,
all alone,
like November in July.
The words danced around Bel's mind off winds
that would have otherwise been hushed to the
ground. Winds silent, waiting for just the right soles
stepping scrumptious into spaces they may or may

not have been ready for. Ready like the times we melted for the sake of what consciousness looks like in a puddle. Puddle. Muddle. Cuddle-in bark skin. Huddle. Shuttle. Subtle-blood filling wood bin. Woods bins carrying melted self for sacrifice to the gods. Gods praying for reason to be. I praying for reason to me. And in this place, in this moment, the girls lost sense of two, and, for ever the slightest of moments felt only one.

If they had been older, it could have, would have, meant something more. Roads building the foundation of things they'd cry about in the mirror so many years later, wondering what it was they had done to deserve the things in life handed to them like hot coals only warm to melt flesh to bone. No more separation. No more separation. Now only the water can cool you. Now only submersion can cure you. Now only can you see the light, shimmering and glimmering through the surface so far above you; so far out of reach.

But hands will still reach out. Fighting even after having made the decision to swim out themselves; ourselves. Humanity drowning for the weight of our myths, our stories, holding us down below the surface. Though at least drowning wasn't a bloody affair. Though, what affairs were worth having that weren't bloody?

Nancy had forgotten Jezebel—or anyone else at all for that matter—was with her, let alone the question she posed what would have been life-times ago if time could be measured in the chaos of the whispers that soaked into her meat in this forest. She smelled the water waiting wistfully for her, though her mind didn't know, some other thing instead now listened to the messages sent. Who are we when our messages become intercepted? Are we anyone at all? When lied to about our own motives? When tied down in our heads with cuffs round wrists loose just enough to remind us it's all real? It's all real when we decide to die.

Bel had planned to talk Nancy out into the water, to see how deep it was, her being too afraid to find out herself. People often talked others out to see the things they feared most. But Bel didn't have to talk Nancy into anything. For as the trees opened up around the ocean, Nancy stepped towards the water's edge with the same determined gait gripping glutinous to her movement since entering the forest's boundaries of the new. Even if only in subtle ways. Maybe, in fact, especially if only in subtle ways. Nancy wondered at how she was different. Wondering, of course, cause she couldn't see how this would play out. Wondered because she couldn't yet tell the world what her death taste like. Like blood in the sand of castles we built our lives out of. One and the same. The same *was* we dreamt as children. One and the same. Like sand castles with blood left behind dripping into calmed water calling our names not in words but in senses intercepted between fire and pain, between water and rain, between cutting out the shapes we saw in magazines once too expensive to wish for from God or any other giver taking the things we paid little mind to and replacing it all with hands holding us under the surface of water pretending to be still.

Still; Nancy carried herself sloshingly out into the dampness of shared dreams.

It flowed quickly, hungrily, into her. Water like blood in veins. Like love in heart. Like thoughts in mind. It slid into and under her skin. Becoming and was. Water pretends all along to give life. Pretending. Just like everything else. But it takes life. The water takes life and we don't notice it. Noticed as fingers searching skin for touch. Noticed like shocks of a system surprised at such; at the touch of fingers and, breath, and . . . water.

Bel watched the water from a dream like perspective. Reality shifts. And we work so hard at shifting it back. At making some sense out of the things made of chaos we reflect from water's surface evolving in every moment; moments of all the one? All the one. But then what happens when the one pulls us down beneath its surface, testing our grit, testing our survival, testing our fucking love for life?

Bel whispered into the air. A word she did not know. A word she could not have repeated if required to. And she would be. In her near future, there was much that would be required of Jezebel.

tumultus

A murmur in the roar of waves tied away from crashing. The desperate hush that rolled along the mirror still surface. Hesitation in the moments lingering in atmosphere between magic and reaction. It's like magic, the way we look at each other when we're about to cum. That stillness in eyes lit fucking aflame from speech and desire of soul. Stillness like water's edge as it cuts in deep. Fingers of the taker of life so, fucking, deep in mind that all becomes only manipulation. God creating universe with the sensual fingertips of water seductively whispering into ears. My dear! My dear,

'Nancy,' was the other thing that Bel hushed through murmured lips as the sight of water, of her friend, gently began to rumble.

It began in Nancy's skin. As feet pulled her lovingly along, further and further out, skin shuddering with the trembles of rumbling water soaked into bones. Skin pulling the strings. Skin the show. Like a pelt of self. A pelt of the strain, suffering, and pure bliss inherent in itself. And the water rumbled too. In sync with the parts swimming in Nancy. A rumbling of 'what's next?' while we ask, magic settles into

rumbling

particles and starts transformation.

A fearful tension gripped at Bel's existence as she stood, watching, wind blowing gently through her hair in ways undefinable, as the rumbling of the scene grew like exponential slow-motion, before her. Something calmed at her, too, at the same time. The mix took charge of her senses. The mix built an anxious arousal in her chest that multiplied and spilled into the rest of her being. She imagined it in her like the water in Nancy. Panic quietly settling in as she feared overwhelming. Overwhelm me. Like water. Like magic. Like panic.

The water overwhelmed Nancy. Only, only she noticed it too late. Or maybe hadn't really noticed *it* at all, but instead the panicked horror that came in notice after; after it was too late. By then body was in control. And body, her body, was being controlled by the desire of water spoken into the real by lips telling stories for gold shavings.

And the water smiled.

And Bel smiled. Lips showing teeth. Intent shared with the world. Share each other. With intent. But, maybe, if done just right it still overwhelms in stillness.

And Nancy let out a whimper.

Jebediah stood in falling sunlight sipping at whiskey in coffee. Sunlight always felt like that; falling, yet still. He liked the sunlight. It felt warm. Felt like it burned away much of the muck that collects on us as we travel through the darkness of night, darkness of the depths of deep sky that somehow taunts eyes, taunts souls. *The Good Lord in the clouds*, Jebediah sighed out in wordless breaths. Pry wasn't 'much' of the muck, but only *some*, that sunlight burned away. Maybe that was our death; muck collectin' at a faster rate than we can burn and wash and rip away. That was only life, he chuckled, 'Faster 'n we can burn and wash and rip away.'

Looking East of his shop-front, Jebediah could see what looked like Jezebel sitting in a daisy field just outside the farthest buildings in town. Eyes scanned feeding brain. Feeding us response, and emotional input faster than we could even consciously track. Sentiment created quicker than process. Was why we couldn't be in each-others' heads. *We* were hardly even making the decisions. Such passionate creatures tied mercilessly to primal response. Maybe it was sexy. Maybe it was terrifying. Maybe it bred chaos in systems that catered more, that cared more, that felt and feel and fear and real . . . more. Those that couldn't as easily edit the system's first response.

Jebediah's first response was angered fear when his eyes failed to find Nancy as they scanned the daisies near Bel. His footsteps fell firm and fast carrying body down dusted road. Bits of shudder found home in his skin, down his spine. He knew he shouldn't have let her go off with that . . . that girl on her own. What with the woods not far outside town. And the water it surrounded. And the smell on them as they came into town only a few days ago. Something off. Some, sourness in the atmosphere around them. But Nancy said Bel was such a sweet girl. Said they were gonna stay nearby. 'This ain't damned nearby,' Jebediah quietly growled as he stomped along towards Bel, towards the daisies . . . towards . . .

'Bel, where's Nancy?' His voice carried ahead of him in the air of the falling sunlight as though a warning of a dog with little bite. Trembled in step. Trembled in the reality of truths Jebediah couldn't possibly have imagined, but yet, knew were real even before his feet, even before words, could reach the little girl sitting in daisy field.

Bel could feel the man approaching. Some, entity, that lived in the spine of her neck twitched at his movement. She knew he'd ask her; asked her things she didn't have the answer for. Something she ought get used to, being asked questions you somehow knew were coming, somehow knew what were, and yet, and yet couldn't for the life come up with an answer to what made any sense. Lost in the question of the universe, mankind was. All only left spinning at the ends of ropes tillin' we had an answer. An answer was the trick. Not *the* answer, but any.

Sunshine kicked through the sky at Bel while Jebediah anxiously shifted weight from side to side.

Sunshine drifting out of the air more and more with each passing moment. Our sunshine fading with blinking eyes. Life like the drifting sight of God before he slips off to sleep and forgets what it was he was thinking when he wakes back up. Or, does he wake from us? Maybe Jezebel's life was only a dream of God. Maybe anyone was. Each only a dream in a moment before eyes open. Open eyes kill us one by one. Bel wondered if Nancy's eyes were open.

'Jezebel,' Jebediah continued on, 'where is Nancy?'

The girl looked up at him with confused eyes. Eyes searching for the right question being asked, of all the marks in the world: 'She went out into the water. I tried telling her she shouldn't . . . but she wouldn't listen to me. Told me to go home if'n I was scared. There's somethin' in those woods, I think. Somethin' scary, sir.'

'You shouldn't have left her in there,' dry lips grimaced out into the very last burning rays of daylight as Jebediah began, in a slow trot at first, (a trot that drove into a full sprint) to run towards the woods. Nancy couldn't swim. His thoughts raced as footsteps fell heavily upon the ground. There's no way she would have gone out into that water. No way. Though, there were all sorts of ways we'd step outside our comfort zone, our normal in the world. Often in the hands of normal being ripped apart. What had Bel said to her? What did she put in her head to get her to go against her own understanding of the *real* around her? We break the real when we need love, when we fear, when we hunger. Maybe they were all the same thing. Maybe it was always all the same thing.

Nancy whimpered as the water overwhelmed her. She knew this was coming. Always knew. Not quite how. Not quite exactly when. But as soon as consciousness gripped onto the situation, situation like a parasite on the universe as its host, she knew this was what she had been feeling all along. All her life, a hanging dread of drowning into the red of her own flowing blood. Blood dripping down already wet legs as evolution into things our loved ones no longer recognize. Recognize me. In a cocoon made from the times lies meant more than pleasant truths. In water made red from the blood of children who didn't realize they'd grown up in the eyes of desire that had waited so patiently for someone to open the door, slide the window, and let 'em in.

Nancy whimpered like water begging to be drunk. Eat me, and drink me. Like fairy tales for bedtime. Bedtime at the bottom of oceans in dreams of God still too excited to yet wake up and so we only linger in the suffering as byproducts of death till the owner decides it can end.

God, let me die like, dragon fly,
caught in spider's web, let me,
high like dragons fly in a,
sky & ocean wed under stars
falling out but called in.
God let me, why under water,
head under cover, and learn the
right way to dream, seam
on the horizon, cream, made of wet skin
skin dripping under the surface again.
God, let me, God before the
spiders dream dreams of gods giving

goosebumps to husbands who knew
passion put children in red water
too deep to climb out of.
Climb out of, like graves
filled in with air.

The water grew a thick flowing red. Red like roses brought to a funeral for family members not dead yet. There's a romance in the way every drop of the hungry water turned a shade of Nancy red as it burst her apart under its surface.

If only we could all have that. If only we could all be burst apart under someone's surface, some thing's, surface, when it's time for God to wake up from the dream called our name. Burst apart in our own desire to never wake up. Becoming the fabric of the others' dreams as the pull of ours dies inside early mornings before gone to work making worlds . . . defining universes. Always carried on. Names in sounds moaned out by lovers brave enough to say what they want. Names in the gently rocking waves of water the world forgot existed till it becomes colored with their childrens' blood. Was what the world was though; noticed when dripping red from the insides of love.

Surely Jebediah found, or could find, no comfort in this having happened time and time again. His life forever tied to blood red water running up over the edges of its own shore. Telling stories we didn't wanna hear. Words that didn't make sense less the audience had suffered the trauma so often given out at birth like consolation prizes in carnivals, like Nancy had once read about. Carnivals made for people to laugh even when they knew they had nothing to laugh at.

The water laughed at Jebediah as he broke

through the rim of trees surrounding its edges, bloodied and scratched from frantic travels. Though he could have taken his time. Taken all the time in the world. She was dead. He knew it the moment Bel had said she went out into the water. Shit, if being honest, he knew it the moment he was born; knew his baby girl was gonna be turned red by magic he couldn't understand, but was victim to nevertheless.

Too often victim to the things that we do not understand. Like how Jebediah just now realized he'd dreamed this scene more times than he could count. Blood in the water. Only, unlike God's, this one wasn't gonna end just because he woke up. No, if anything our nightmares only intensified when woken into blood red water. The town would be drinking his daughter, Jeb thought, after the next hard rain.

And he fell to his knees sobbing. Unable to forgive himself for his dreams.

CHAPTER 3
DUST TRAILS TO OUR CHILDREN

JEBEDIAH WAS SORROWFUL for things he couldn't explain. He sifted through the water that day. The light having faded entirely. Like love lived lifetimes ago. And replaced by the same subtle orange hue of dreams little girls lived through pretending they were asleep. How much of life did we pretend to sleep through? Whispers in the dark from lips that felt more comfortable if they could say without having to admit. Admit self to the other. Though, probably, harder still to admit self to self. So we dream instead. We dream of oceans reddened from the flesh of our life. We dream of touch we can't admit. We dream of self we won't say. But will let darkness say for us. Pretending naivety in the morning light, trying its best to eat away that ominous hue that lingered and followed no matter the work we did to keep it at bay.

There was nothing left of her. Nothing left but blood-soaked water. Not a stitch of clothing, thought Jebediah. Not a stitch of flesh to ever suggest he had once had a daughter. Only his tears as evidence that there was ever a before before now. So hard to let go of such tears. When they feel they are all we have left. When they feel like anchors that give us ground to mean something or anything, really at all. If looking closely, closely enough, one could see the silent silhouette of a young girl in the teardrops running for their lives down Jebediah's face. It was a beautiful suggestion of a memory that would one day fade away into a sentence or two. It all fades away with enough time. Though they'll never admit it.

The rest of the town followed a mourning used-to-be father into the woods the next day. None being willing to go such places in the dark of night. None able to even get out of Jebediah a single word for hours and hours after he finally stumbled back out of the water, back out of the woods. He had been scratched up badly from fumbling in the dark hue of dark dreams that could not have been woken from. And was stained a blood red wet that he was unable to give voice or reason to till daylight finally broke the surface of the morning sky. When he finally spoke up, finally said word, it carried a weight that wouldn't make full sense in the moment: 'She took her under the water.' Words aching with life they'd forever miss. 'My little girl is dead.'

It didn't take much to collect nearly everyone in town on the way back out to water, red from disappeared. The state of Jebediah created a buzz like bees busy at work that night that ran wild as flames from dry deserted heat. The plains surrounding them ablaze in metaphor that no one could possibly ignore. Metaphor being all. Metaphor being the definition of the human experience. Without, all only animals looking for food and fuck and a covering overhead.

Though maybe that's all things were, even while saturated in the metaphor handed us by a God who misplaced trust in what we are capable of. Capable of blood in the water. Capable of blood in our love.

The water was still red when they slowly emerged, hesitant to disbelieve, from trees most had never set foot in. Even brighter, maybe, than the night before, under Jebediah's neglectful sight. Was it the daylight that made the red shine so much brighter than before? Daylight that made all our pain shine brighter than the last? Or had the water become even more red? Maybe Nancy was held somewhere, under the surface, slowly bled dry, more and more, bit by ocean bit, into a water with pretense at innocence, but was in truth a monster hungry for all the insides it could lure from solid ground. The sea calling us back. Escaped for only but a time then dragged back through blood to our home. Come home to me. And die like good little children.

Jebediah imagined for the briefest of moments the water rising up in red waves and crashing down upon all the audience he himself was responsible for gathering. A brief moment that then became the rest of his life. As so many of our imagined moments do become. Become. We become the things we can't help but thinking. Those ones we didn't mean but that somehow mean us even before thought forms. Noticed like lives we couldn't live before we die.

'Look!' he called out all around, 'look what it has done to my little girl! Look,' eyes searching the crowd, 'at what *she* has done!' But *she*, Bel, he could not find. Her kin neither. Were they there? Somewhere in the sea of faces that once looked familiar to him and now

41

only seemed ghosts on a shore of his own tragedy? Hiding away with grins and laughter as their contorted expression? Or did they stay back, kept away from the nightmare brought to town with dusted footsteps like any other? Hidden in plain sight. Weren't we all? Hidden in plain sight? Waiting for a moment to slip our existence through the cracks in others' and be as though we had always been. Dreaming like dying ghosts who've forgotten how to swim till the water is thick enough with blood that they float to the top in a muck that would become the ground footsteps carried life onto. Jebediah would never dream again. But only die each time eyelids closed and remind him of the life taken by living. They'd feign compassion. Wasn't real though. Never is, in truth. In truth they were just glad it wasn't their children who died, who disappeared, or whatever else may have happened to poor Nancy that night. It wouldn't settle in till their own dreams spread through consciousness like a disease destined to turn their whole town into a blood red mist growing nightmares of the future. A future born from non-waking gods tired from pretending.

All, slowly, tired of pretending. The things hidden under the show constantly trying, deeper, quicker, sleeker, slicker, to eat their way out. The reality binding, binding, binding me, binding you, binding us to true, even if it bleeds through like stuck pigs waiting to feed to die to live a life of starstuff telling stories like wild west myths in a setting we don't recognize any more. Can't recognize for all the blood and tears that cover every surface. A thick grime that reminds us of the places in history our programming promises us we've been. But is there any proof? Is there any proof that Nancy ever existed? Is there any proof that any of them did? Them, being the children of the town, the other children who, after Nancy disappeared into blood red lake, one by one became sick.

Sick like dying from the get go.
Dying to let go.
Dying. Like sick from trying
to tow the line
fine blooded
fly blooded
insect in the mind, and we find
from flying forward further & further into fire
as desire of things told we shouldn't want
that the scars hurt worse than
the cuts ever could
even as, children begging mother
people begging lover,
each other to, touch in the darkness of
spinning universe, disgraced, due
to
black hole
you, black hole desire in
with the gravity of
gravity doves flutter by in
pure romance.
Pure romance
chance given to
love like parents loving children
sick from magic they'll only magic too late.
Magic too late to save their world so instead
dead, instead, led astray into witch's brew,

me and, you, loved together in
finger-tip embrace graced cover of never ending
story teller.

Never ending storyteller. Of a tale as old as time.
The decay of flesh. For the townsfolk could only
pretense so long. Happy it wasn't their own. Because
before they could even take it for granted; their
children became sick and died.

It happened so quick but not quick enough. Each
individual tragedy self-contained and not. Like panic
attacks telling mind it's fine but it's dying, into a new
space where existence is defined by endless
overwhelming. They were pulled into the walls of
their sorrow by hands unseen but seen unfelt but felt
unmoved but moved. A time constrained by a spell
that held them tight in the one moment: the moment
of their own despair. Felt like it was coming forever.
Building, grown like moss on stone. Destiny in a
pained death that none of them could avoid. Nothing
avoided. Even trying our best. Even trying the rest
when the first over and over and over and over again
didn't solve it. But the rest only felt like the best way
to hurt on the way to the grave. They all had dreams,
each in their first night of the sickness, some coming
the day after, others the day after that and the day
after that. By a week after Nancy red night, a quarter
of the parents in town had only bloody bedding and
stained floors as evidence their children ever were.
Memories overridden like rats in the cellar. Their
minds becoming only a mist.

Their dreams haunted them as much as the cries
for 'please! please mama! please papa! make it stop!
make it *blood vomit in bucket over rim like lake over

ocean*!' Dreams of an attic with red mist tint hiding orange hue of moonlight laughing at heartache. A werewolf feeling of transformation in skin. Insides pushing out beyond their borders. Borders meant to be ripped apart so we can grow into new spaces. But the metaphor couldn't supersede the reality. If that was in fact what this was, their new reality forcing itself like a rapist in a horse barn with hand over mouth in prickling hay that will never feel like memories again. Missing Sunday. Sunday being the day of the weak where the most children seemed to succumb to the magic making them die, as magic as the magic of life.

Hands couldn't clean as quickly as red rushed from their little bodies. Though they tried. They all tried. They all always try to clean up their death, their sadness. It was maybe the quintessential human myth. Trying to clean up the mess of what it was like to be alone together in this sharp-filled existence. Together like wild animals still pretending God loves them best. How can she love us, when we're so covered in blood? Vomiting up on ourselves from dreams we refuse to acknowledge overlap so with each other till we see the looks on their faces as they emerge from doorways into the open world and sob collectively in a sunlight pretending at nourishment. We need to die to live. But . . . does it really have to hurt so much? Do we really have to be so helpless in the process?

Helpless to save children from a dark magic that must be out to only satisfy itself. Though maybe we too were that dark magic. What energy was eaten for the little ones to breathe without choking on bubbles of their own blood? What cost of tears in the universe? What privilege to be here, breathing dusted air, even in pain, for but a brief instant in what we so define as time.

Sickness takes us all. Young and old. Whether we watch for it or not. Whether prescribed by witches disguised as just another face in the crowd or not. Whether we lock ourselves away or not. Death slips in through the cracks we can't possibly seal up tight. For fear of suffocating under little girl water, crying itself into blood red tears of self. There is no sorrow like sorrow. Didn't matter if it was dusted on the trail. The town cried their tears. And inside two weeks of misted night mourning, more children were only stains in lives than not. The ones still fearing death locked up tight in their homes with frantic families terrified they couldn't stop what was yet to come.

And then trauma led to anger.

And chants started slowly under breath.

They weren't even people anymore.

How could they be? Having lost that one thing which truly made them feel as something more than teeth growling in the darkness of the universe. The only white bone that would dull and fade with time and blood and screams. Not only children. So many creatures had that. Had reproduction. But love. Love in that human way. Maybe not so different or unique from the love of other species floating around with us in this muck world, spurting filth off all of us into the infinite. But different somehow. Muckier . . . somehow. A love that might kill in revenge as equaled as defense. A love that built worlds. Maybe the love that built this world. Though that would mean these blood stains and blood streaks on used-to-be father, mother, skin, had all been built in the world created through love. *How was this love?* every one of them thought simultaneously in complete and utter isolated loneliness. Nothing like that loneliness. Of hurting in existence. The trauma of the rational brain turned off so the traumatized brain could turn on. Solely. We are all the sole owners of sorrow. Each better and harder than the last. Thinking more than the next but there never is a next. Only more of the same. Only more of the 'how do I get through this night, again?' More of the why. Not why did this or that happen. We knew, deep down we knew that it was well deserved for the sin of our lives. But why bother carrying on? The human spirit championed for its resilience. Pathetic in truth. Addiction in truth. We, so addicted to tragedy, that we refuse to smile other than when hiding tears, and refuse to die when there's more good suffering to be had.

Good suffering. As opposed to the bad suffering. Good suffering like dead children dragged through the dusty road so all could see the play of our pain and sorrow. Good suffering. As opposed to bad. Some suffered better than others. But deciding which was which was hard. Hard like I want to watch you under dimmed light. Hard like I want to watch you under the brightness of magma explosion in space time. Hard like I want to be the space time you melt away into. Hard like:

Noah watched his mother prepare him just a bit of tea. He knew it must be something fairly serious, that he had, because Mother's tea was, 'Only for special occasions,' as she had told him so many times, being that it came from so far away and took so much to get. Was a better way to say than cost. A more honest way to weigh what it is the universe takes from us for the cost of existing. It takes so much.

'Is,' Noah coughed hard, a fit that grew into minutes must'a been, 'it . . . (and again) . . . is it a special occasion Mother?' The moments seemed like many over the last couple days. Agony at helplessness in watching loved ones simply get worse. Like watching us go crazy. Like watching self go crazy inside your head, up close and personal. Only this wasn't crazy. This was dying. Isola knew it. Her little boy was dying. The stench of death was already heavy in the town from moments just like these, for others. Duplicate spaces in time. Duplicate tragedy. A darkness hung over our own despair. A triviality. Even our sorrow wasn't unique. Though still lonely. It was the dichotomy we all had to live with, live through; our tragedies were multiplied millions of times all over humanity and yet isolated us as burrowed stones in hardened rock skidding along the empty spaces in God's plan. We rumbled round rather silently in the parts of the story that happened on their own while the creator spent focus on other things, other details. So often that was how this life felt, occurrence in detail as creator spent time on things that were in detail not us. How could it not be lonely as we die? How could Noah not feel lonely as he bled to death from the inside out? How could Isola not feel alone in watching him leave her? His father gone since before this began.'It is, my sweet darling, it is.' She held back the tears in what seemed an effortless effort. A professional. Who held back the trembling in ways that made skin hardly noticeable at all. Though it rippled on her in waves of anxiety from all the bottled-up life that constantly wanted to boil over. One day. Soon enough. That voice whispered in her head as she walked towards Noah's bed with expensive Chinese tea. He would die and she could break apart, finally, fully. A pang of guilt at, maybe, in a roundabout sort of way, being relieved at having the excuse to crumble away, to let, herself wash into the waves of eternity. In that Isola felt nearly as responsible as the witchcraft that was surely at fault for all this. God wouldn't allow such things. And so it must have been something unnatural at hand. But her sickness in death made her deserve. 'We all deserve this don't we?' she mumbled under breath, holding in tears from concerned child eyes.

'What, Mother?'

And she only grinned, 'Nothing, dear. Carefully now, it's hot,' as she handed him the cup. Steam streaming into the air from rim, waiting for tender lips. Streaming up and dissipating past perception in particular patterns of once upon a time I used to be. Just like our deaths. Whether subtle or not. All collected up into the one shared moment. A collective death of but a million individual moments. And which shall you be? Doesn't matter. One in the same. Two in the same. Three. No one noticed least it be their own flesh returned to dust from whence it came. And even then, noticed for such a brief time as to hardly be a time at all. Isola knew that. She knew that her son's death would eventually be but a distant memory on a timeline of remembering human.

No. That wasn't true.

This would be her forever. Missing him until maybe one day, if day it could be called, their energies came to share the same space again. No matter the duration of this life called death.

Noah felt nausea for an instant, as his mother reached to hand him a cup, an instant before blood red seeped past lips like the tide in trees then gushed out of his mouth, covering blanket again. 'Oh God, my baby . . . ' Isola dropped the cup, it shattering and adding tea to fluids already building memories in floor boards, no longer concerned with its exotic origins, and probably, in truth, having never been concerned with them to begin with. She held him, with trembling terrified hands that only wished their loving touch could somehow overpower like magic the magic that darkened what once felt like her home and now only felt like a nightmare. Her words whispered to him that everything was going to be okay. It was a lie. She knew. And he knew too.

We know these lies. See and are desperately familiar with their faces. The way their eyes twinkle. And we let them comfort us. Need them to comfort us. Noah needed that comfort. So too did his mother, Isola. Comfort in 'everything is going to be okay' both given and received. We need to believe we can comfort one another. As needed as the air lungs breath, as the water body drinks. It's the only hope there is. Hope at its foundation.

Noah died about an hour later. Isola's still clutched embrace surrounding his limp, wet body. He felt lighter. That's when she knew, before notice of breath, before notice of heartbeat, that he had gone; the weight of life no longer filling his little body. He'd been seven years old. His favorite color was a deep, forest green. A natural tone. A natural tone like the screams his mother refused herself knowing she would have to bury her son . . . And would never get blood stains out of wood, out of memory. Stuck forever in the same instant of the world. Over and over like train stuck on a circular track. Over and over again like . . . like witches poisoning the world with casual death like casual sex like casual love like casual desire. Burning down the world one town at a time. But why? Isola cried out in finally tears. Tears that missed for longer than this current shell could remember. Why did her child have to die? Why did any of them? Why did all of them?

It was the same in more homes. Not all, but nearing so so quickly. They say that's how these sorts of things spread, quickly, but this seemed even to move faster than that. Though in the moments, they felt forever. It felt like forever watching our children cry tears of I'm-gonna-die right before eyes filled with something kin to pretense of hope. But maybe that was all hope ever was, had ever been, was pretense, was a pretense in the world of the world. Hope spreading so much slower than disease. Humanity like a communicable disease of consciousness in the universe, spreading from one to the other in an endless stream of blood flowing as water, water flowing as air, air flowing as being. What are we now but the leftovers? What is this but the shell of things left behind as we try to live through life not meant for living in the first place? It is the sorrow we are forced to find nourishment in as penance for spreading like sickness. Life, only an imagined thing minds made up in response to how bodies shiver and shake in the moonlight of night, in the absence of day.

But that wasn't exactly true. Not exactly true since this sickness wasn't only that, even should it seem to behave as such. Behaving as such and being as such being oh so different. And they knew. They knew this wasn't something so simple.

Maybe it had been the disappearance of Nancy that predicted this space which gave them a sense something else was at hand. The blood in the water. The taste in the air. Or maybe they'd just needed something to blame.

We so often needed blame.
So often needed, same to see
self in something like
starlight fight-
ing for attention,
fighting for feeling like fighting.
Or maybe then we lose pretense.
Then we lose starlight hope that it's
'not us' who's dying but only
someone else trying to
be things they've not been allowed
in so, so long. Allow me to, bleed
nourishment into you.
Allow for true make believes
to give us a direct line to God.
God.
How could she let this happen?
How could she let me happen?
Us?
This?
This, pain in head like

THEY BUILT A GALLOWS FOR YOU AND ME

dead brain matter
giving hats to Hatters
making bellies fatter
for fresh fire feeding frozen fragments fragmented
first and last in the creations we cry to sleep in.
To sleep in . . .
To sleep in me like witchcraft hungry for
something that's not in the house,
mouse and man telling stories to
one up each other.
This town, this death, was up
plus one, for finders keeping
losers weeping
monsters sleeping,
in the day so they can run rampant at night.
Night.
Please.
How it transforms in the night.
How they transform in the night.
To become the unbearable. The unbearable.
Like unwearable faces for the lies they hide
and seek with flashlights only to light
their way.
But the way isn't lit,
for the right people,
with light but with shining blood
seeping through cuts in flesh to get the calm
get the calm
get the calm
even in the madness.
It was madness how they died.
Madness how we died. Together.
Waiting to be hung for our sins.

Slowly, as the bodies built up, grief found blame in the only way it could: in the new: in the unfamiliar. In the puddles of their own children's blood the townsfolk began to see the faces of the family come unexpectedly to town. Of Ma most significantly. It was Jezebel who'd been with Nancy, sure, but youth somehow always got a pass. Even if there had been something in her, they collectively thought by themselves, *she* must have put it there. Maybe it was what had been taken from them, the innocence of their own children, but in the crimson hue of personal darkness we can't even lay claim to it only being how desire responds to rejection. The town decided within themselves that *she* had been the cause of their children's' death. And she must, of course, pay.

'For their rock *is* not as our Rock, even our enemies themselves *being* judges. For their vine *is* of the vine of Sodom, and of the fields of Gomorrah: their grapes *are* grapes of gall, their clusters *are* bitter: Their wine *is* the poison of dragons, and the cruel venom of asps. *Is* not this laid up in store with me, *and* sealed up among my treasures? To me *belongeth* vengeance, and recompence; their foot shall slide in *due* time: for the day of their calamity *is* at hand, and the things that shall come upon them make haste. For the Lord shall judge her people, and repent herself for her servants, when she seeth that *their* power is gone, and *there is* none shut up, or left. And she shall say, Where *are* their gods, *their* rock in whom they trusted . . . ?'

Nothing like sorrow focused sharp to a point held with certain quivering hands up gently to throat. Nothing like it except when it's our own throats the spear is pointed at. But that couldn't be? Could it? We could never be the cause, the orchestrator of our own demise . . . could we? Were we? In Bel's mother did the other mothers only see themselves reflected back at them? Did that make it easier? Easier to instantly hate her because they'd been secretly hating themselves in their own skin for so long without words or reasons or excuses. Finally now they could hate that, and they had an excuse, and it almost felt . . . nay, it *did* feel, so good. It felt good in that relief type of way. It felt good like the way it felt good to hurt one's self. It felt good in the emptiness of autopilot at no longer having to explain but instead being allowed to only feel. I want to only feel. And leave the rest alone. They wanted to feel. And so they chanted, under breath at first, then louder, and louder, day after day, after, one death adding up to the next, and so on, till eventually like choir of saddened anger, from nearly every home peppering the town's land could be heard the screams of, 'WITCH!'

Like crying to be seen in this empty world. Dying to be remembered in the moments before our death. They couldn't be forgotten. Why? Why . . . we seem to never know. Maybe because we've forgotten already. Maybe we never remembered from the start. Maybe, really, forgetting was the point. Having the courage to be forgotten, overlooked, left out in the rain for 30 days and 30 nights with fears that we built arks protected by guards who'd never let us on. Our own savior not for us. Our own safety slipped away by waters we knew were coming but couldn't possibly have planned for. Did they plan to die by candlelight while bodies still breathed breaths that had been tired before this even got started? They did not. Die, they did not. But only told stories of so as to have an excuse for the smell of burnt flesh that would, if hope delivered, soon enough scent the mist they called sky . . . the mist they called life.

Revenge, not for loss, but for birth of something to lose. For simply being. Each and every one of us. And in that they intended Ma to pay for all their sins. We always did. Only telling stories so that it seemed okay. Maybe that was true. Maybe it didn't matter, matter much; death had been brought to their town in buckets too small to hold it for long, and it seeped over edges before rushing round ankles in a flood of unanswered prayers.

CHAPTER 4
BURN THE WITCH

CAN FEEL THEM COMING. Always can. Always can feel them coming like the sadness of dark, like the inevitability of decay, like wind in leaves. It grinds at you in slow steady footsteps, crowd doing the best it can to move in unison. Justifies action somehow. If we all move the same. Feels right. Feels like destiny. When our sadness sings the same song. Some comfort in knowing we are not the only ones. But we are. Aren't we? Even playing at another hollow face in the crowd. There is no crowd. Only illusion. Only pretense at same but . . . but . . . but reckon if that's the best we can come up with then what else can be done? What more can comfort but the simple desire to be comforted?

Which was why their footsteps pulled them along with minds hardly even thinking any more. Reacting instead like animals fighting for the last scraps of forgiveness dangling as strips of red flesh from the sides of the dinner table. It was nourishment until we died. It was nourishment until God decided the game was over. Give up your turn. Give up the ghost. So the next rider has something with which to call their own.

Something to call home. For a while. Till it realizes what must be paid for that and decides to skip town in a buggy drawn by horses who've been taught to move like mime silence. Silence because to make sound is to be, and to be gives some credibility to the horrible sounds that people make when filled with nothing but panic, panic and shame, shame at the sounds they've come startlingly to realize are coming from their very own mouths.

Feed ghost into mouth to be happy again. Feed the leftovers to quiet the horses. So's to not have anything left to tempt hungry townsfolk looking to fill holes in them left from forgetting to eat as they watched their children bleed to death. If I bleed to death will you watch me? Will you say something? Will you sing to me? Or will you hide away with mouth covered, peeking out every now and then to make sure you're not close enough to catch whatever it is what has my skin thrashing about in blood-soaked sheets from the tears slipping through pores in flesh cut open by whispers of the world so we don't have to admit it was *us* that did it all along? Shhhh . . . There'll be none of that talk in this, our Great Southern Witch Hunt, for we've already made certain in our heads who it is that's to blame for these, our deepest of misfortunes. And even that was lie. The state of things couldn't possibly be passed off as misfortune. Will. Or witch. Or wind. There was never any missing of fortunes that we couldn't have paid attention to in the first place. Lost for fear of being found. Found out.

So instead, crowds are formed and announcements are made so the causes will know, without a doubt, that their judgement is coming, even without understanding what that judgment was, what it meant, and just how hungry it could be.

Bel could feel them coming. Like Ma had taught her. But she couldn't understand what it meant. Too young to know the sharpness of their teeth filed down forcibly fine for flesh to fall gently down stained throats. Too young to know it was *her* they came for. And really, they too didn't know this, not just yet. Sure, there was grumble in the ranks, but even parents maddened with grief couldn't set out to punish children for that which they could not judge properly without their creator supporting them with signs that read what direction to head in. Especially when that grief was written out in the blood of their little ones, still, in some instances, warm and wet on the floors and bedding of their own homes.

Something extra in the pain we bring so close to ourselves, the pain we paint our homes in, ourselves in; it weighs on us in ways that makes our cries sound like lost in space, like screams caught and soaked up by starlight that couldn't have cared less about astral coordinates and signs written in ether by God trying to keep some level of learn-your-lessons in the chaos pretending at the things we have figured out. They only wanted to die. But couldn't. Instead deciding that misery loves company, so come decay with me, and if you're lucky, we can make your rate just a bit faster.

Though it's gonna hurt.

It always hurts.

Always too much like make it end please but no one is listening. All too busy gettin' by. All too busy lovin' life, lovin' lie, to do much beyond stand by and watch cry me a river to drown you in. Always and never again. Cause this is the last time. The last time a town marched towards one home like this, with this much bile in silent steps. Well, there was no last time like this, it being the first and only, so if'in you wanna watch, best put your coin down and get in line like the rest of us waiting to see what comes next.

But the seats fill up quick. So make your decision. And stop talking so as the show can begin. Begin just like again and again we've played this part and it always gets so damned bloody as soon as we start that all those who ain't involved step away and find something to keep themselves busy, for fear of it being so much more than they ever bargained for. Bargain for the smell first. The words come after. Or not at all. If lips is what they came for. If feet stomped through voice lookin' for something to silence cause that was even more romantic than death. Death a romance of alone in the stars with nothing left to say.

Pa had went away on business two days prior. Francis begged him to stay. But he couldn't. Said so. They'd moved here so quickly, there were things left behind he had to manage. Or that's what he said. What grownups were always saying, always talking about, the things they had to, could, couldn't, manage. Made Francis wonder if she were just another thing Pa had to manage in his life. And if so, what was the point of all of it. Sign up like extra credit for a test never taken. Sign up like manage things never signed up for.

He didn't listen though. Sure he pretended. Sure he'd say he listened if asked. But he didn't really. Not really, Francis thought. So how could he know? How could he know of the things Francis had to manage without actually giving her the time?

'I want you to stay, Pa.'

'Can't darling. But I won't be gone long. Maybe a week.'

She looked down at the floor. Floor always pulling us in those, I don't wanna, spaces. Hard to look you in the eye through tears again. Wanting to but not wanting to. Hard looking life in the eye sometimes . . . most times, probably. 'I don't like it here. It's scary.'

'Scary?' His eyes pulled at her. She could feel it without looking. 'What's scary about it?' What's scary about it? What's scary about life? Existence in the void. That's what it was. Constant. Always. No matter who we were, no matter age or interaction, existence was existence in the void. And the only thing there was to give comfort was the perceptions of connection to other perceptions. And when they leave, when they're gone? Well we feel lonely. We feel lost. Like existence before there was. Too little do people prescribe the weight of what loneliness really is. The worst thing in the universe. The reason why God created. Reason why we did in the likeness of. Our creation, ultimately being the mythos of who we were, who we are, to each other. But how could Francis explain that to her father?

So instead, 'They feel sick, Papa. The people here. They smell lonely.'

'They smell lonely do they?' He smiled at his little girl, because of his little girl. Wondering at exactly what her mind meant by the thought, by the expression. The maze of complexity that was the thought machine creating reality as it goes inside her head. Inside all our heads was the similar , yet entirely different. And while it hadn't occurred to him; there was a smell to loneliness, wasn't there?

'Yes, Pa, they do.' Smell like surrounded by hands that didn't exist. Only but the sense of self gripping at self. The smell of disconnect. But why fear it? Fear it like the smell of sickness? Fear it like plague in tired eyes? Looking sickness in the eye was kin to looking the mortality of material being in the eye, and seeing self submerged like under water of reality ready to make-believe red mist swirling round wrists made of fabric cut to form sunspots.

Are we the same as sunspots imagining themselves as people?

'Well, darlin', you ain't gotta be scared cause ya got your mother here, and your sister and little baby brother to keep ya from fallin' victim to the loneliness of these folks while I'm gone.' A comforting tone.

A comforting tone that even her young response to the world felt guilty at not being comforted by, not really: 'What if they come for me?' There was a disquieting certainty in the sound of fear as she stated the question. Question that wasn't really question at all.

He looked deep at her. Squinting in the atmosphere of melancholy at wanting to be reassuring, and knowing that that reassurance was for *us* as much as whomever it wasthat heard words spoken aloud like praying to self, hoping our divine was also listening. To reassure meant there was reassurance. And we needed that. 'Francis, ain't nobody coming for you, okay?' She nodded. Still looking down. 'Hey, look at me,' she did as told, eyes up as brows lowered in trying gaze, 'no one is comin' for you Francis. Long as I'm breathing air.'

And that was that. They both pretended that she felt better bout him goin'. But she hadn't. So often we stumble into the same space. Both as given and received. Hard to know what to do in those moments, those scenes. Instead of deciding something real, we decide to pretend. And maybe that was the real, was as real as people could hope to get to. Hope. Again. That word that could not be avoided when praying in the witchcraft of the human tragedy, the human comedy.

Maybe the town knew Pa was headed out as their reasoning built towards 'Burn the witch' while making their own decisions at pretense of playing the roles our universes gave to us. Maybe not. Maybe each of us knew the story somewhere deep enough in our bones that we couldn't remember it until after it already happened. Something about hindsight. Something about looking over one's shoulder as traveling along through space. Watching it all unfold backwards and knowing, then, that it was the same as when we were headed into it, only lying to self so we could act like we hadn't been here before. But we had; we had and we would. That was the feeling of loneliness. That was the feeling of knowing they'd come for you. Knowing it would be in the darkness. Knowing it would be in the illumination of torch light cackling as burnt air around disaster. The only surprise was why we couldn't say as it unfolded. Unfolded into itself in the exact same way as always.

There were perfectly good reasons to be scared, to be fearful, to be fear-filled: they were coming, for

Francis or otherwise: they were coming and no comfort would stop them.

Hurting as preparation for disconnect. We felt it in the mirror as we watched self make decisions that seemed there was no way around. Though knew there was. Knew that all we had to do was to decide differently, decide control. Was that the truth? Did the townsfolk decide outside their homes in the dark holding torches, that this was the space they wanted to be in? Or did they only find themselves there, led by events set in motion the moment motion first set in, with no way around, over, nor under. Only through. The only way out is through. With no way to know how close to the end till much after we've been through it, and on to the next moment in which to live. Was the cycle of things. Was the inevitability of all the same at all the time. Every moment the same as the next. No matter how restless grown. No matter how anxious in the static of the lives we'd not built but had been built for us by another, by *the* other. But if it were all the one then it was us at the end, facing self with open arms, wondering why it had taken so long, why it had been so hard.

But this hadn't been so long. This was what felt like immediate. This was quicker than a breath of air while not paying attention. Quick like rip the scab off and watch it bleed before even blood flows out into the atmosphere. They'd reached nearly the doorstep. And what as knock? What *as* notice that it was time? Tick tock tick tock, clock watching events unfold with which to judge itself by.

A torch flew through the air. It swirled like an acrobat poorly paid to entertain folks even poorer than display of grandeur, tumbling with perfection, before THUD against the door, followed by gentler THUD against porch step below. It carried a force that was just ever so strong enough to say hello in tones that dared be answered. But not much more. Ma ignored it, though she heard, they all heard it. And something in them, each, in different ways, knew precisely what it was they were hearing, maybe not in specifics, but in the fundamentals of the scene they were just about to play out through perfectly choreographed trauma, the sorts most folk would bury deep in self and let rot away while staring into the void of their very own walls drinking tears so as to not wake in the night thirsty for touch. They all stayed in their own quiet lull, waiting to see what would take off first. That was where it existed; in the waiting. Waiting like babies not touched by mothers, too busy in fields finding time to spend time on, for someone to, if they could only, brush fingertips along skin to make them feel alive so many years later. Make them feel alive like remembering the loneliness of high plains in minds tightened by too much; too much of it all.

And as they waited, as Ma ignored, or, really, pretended to ignore; another THUD struck the door, this time followed by, 'Come out witch!'

There it was, Ma thought. She smelled it in the sickness affecting the young ones. Turn to the unknown first. They'd decided in their own chatter that if she came willingly they'd spare the rest, even with the taint of witchcraft on their skins. It was mother who taught us to lie, after all, and so however it was they came to the conclusion in their own grief, their own sadness, it was Ma they knew was the cause of this deadly magic which overtook their once peaceful and normal home.

'Come out witch! And confess your sins! Or we'll take the children first, same as you took ours!' Same but different, she thought as tears welled in her eyes searching for what to do. Eyes looking out window so timid to be found out, to be found feeling. Don't show them. It's too hard. Too hard to show, to let anyone, anything, in. Easier to deny. Easier to sit quietly and let others tear themselves apart trying to decode our intent, our motive, our thoughts and feelings as we watched angry mob beg for our frangibility, beg to let them mean enough to see us break apart. Than to speak out. Even at,

even at(?),

even at such a cost.

And she refused, in her silence. She refused knowing that the men and women who stood outside her home would come in, would take her Jezebel, her Francis, maybe even baby James, and tie them tightly to the stake already planted deep in ground. She refused for reasons that even here are too hidden to be known. Had she not believed them, it would have made more sense. But she did. She heard it in their eyes that their hearts had been broken. They had nothing left to mend. Human went away. Instead left with the anger and grief of loss. A hungry, savage animal that could not be sated but thought it could be. The worst kind. Or best. Depending, reckon, on what one needed from it.

If their hunger was insatiable, however, then what point was there in feeding them? Was it even worth addressing? Or instead protect life as can be and hope the carnage wasn't too painful in the process? Let them feed as they will. Let their bellies fill long enough to distract. And live on with self intact?

No. No. Surely she couldn't have believed they'd take innocent children in her own stay. Surely she couldn't have trusted to let sad wolves. But what was spoken as she negotiated through cries and screams of hurt animals with nothing left to protect? What was spoken as she cried in terror, clutching her precious children while the collective prepared their judgement in the darkness beyond?

The saddest moment is realizing the only one preventing our suicide is ourselves.

Mary looked down at the dirt below her feet that seemed to shimmer in the light of the fire like ocean under surface of the moon. Warmed to be a part of this mob. Torches in hands. Was like a story written in the earth we walked on. Mary wanted to smile at that. She liked the idea of our lives being some sort of story in the trail of life itself. But, this story was dark and sad. And so very hard to tell, to live. Sometimes admitting to self just how difficult it has been is kin to opening the flood gates of all we held back. Simply saying, yes . . . it was terrible, made it such so much more. Opened the door to our hurt, our tears, our hands on heads searching for heart to stop thinking so we can sleep again, can breathe again. Life lived breathing other people's breath. Till they look away to whisper spells deep into the darkness. Whisper us away. Like dying children.

No, Mary could not smile at any of this.

'Burn her!' she heard yells that pulled her back

from thoughts of . . . thoughts of . . . all the darkness. Didn't they see it? Didn't any of them see it? Did she? She was here after all, wasn't she? Same as the rest? With what intent? The intent of confession from this witch woman? Forgiveness? To kill her? Was that the motivator all along, to kill this woman in front of her children? Or, or the children themselves?

Was that what they wanted?

Was that, what *she* wanted?

More yells pulled her again. Something sounded like Ben in the distance. Her poor Ben. How he looked at her. Dying from this sick. Dying from this curse. Not saying much. Only eyes pleading with his comfort to make it better. We plead with our comfort. Oh won't you make it better? Can't you, please? He looked at her like that. And she couldn't. Now she heard him here and it brought his face to her mind's eye. A vision in . . . what? Memory. Melody. Remember when. Used to be. What is the thought of the dead? Especially as so recent. Could it still be the ones we have lost? Residual like the burn in air after burn in superstition. And as she smelled the residue of burning memory, she knew it was too late here for question. Question had been abandoned in this place. This place lit by sorrow in flames.

The door had burst open.

Mother screamed.

She really did.

But, there were too many.

And the way they looked at James.

'PLEASE! Spare him!'

It was all she could do.

It was all she could do.

Jezebel had known what was going to happen. She dreamed this all before. But she cried anyway. Again. The townsfolk took her and Francis from their home. They came for them after all. Always after all. Even though Pa had said they weren't. Even when the world said, everything was gonna be alright, we knew otherwise, didn't we? Bel knew Pa lied to Francis. That he believed it? Did it make it any less lie? Probably not. Probably not.

Francis called out for her parents as they pulled her and Bel out front. They, dragging Ma out shortly after. The rope binded round the girls tight, squeezing their screams nearly shut as hands, dozens, hundreds, thousands tied them to the stake grown in the ground as always been. It hurt. But what it made Bel smell was even worse than the discomfort. Tears dripped down her young face. She couldn't see Ma, but heard as someone shoved her hard towards the earth. Maybe she dropped baby James. He was crying too hard through it all to tell one way or the other. Life had the tendency to do that; burn us at the stake so often it was hard to tell if the smell was flesh or only memories of tears burning alive. Baby brothers wrapped in the harsh embrace or dirt cover. Cover in dirt like cover in shell. Cover each other in a love that we thought might shield from torches. Was that true? Did Mother fight at all for them?

But of course; questions were long burned away.

An orange fire hue took over the sky as two men wearing hoods like masks lit the hay bunched round Francis and Jezebel's feet. The girls' screams were only but a part of the orchestra of their sacrifice. Roaring along with the eating of the flames. Their skin took in heat first, before flame leapt up. No pleasant glow in horrified fear. It burned in char before their eyes could count, and almost subtly danced upwards, like passionate lover with anxious hands, along their bodies.

You couldn't hear their screams over,
chanting coming from crooked mouths,
'Burn the witch! Burn the witch! Burn the witch!'
. . . Witches, thought their mother. She couldn't watch them burn. But they wouldn't let her look away. So instead, in silence, in panicked breaths, she whispered clouded eyes, and imagined dancing with her husband, the children playing somewhere just out of frame of sight, in a beautiful field of sun, the sound of laughter and gently running water just in the background; trees singing in exhales through tall grass telling each other secrets. If she told it, she could make it so. Wasn't that the reality of things? But, even her whispers couldn't take her from the scene. Hard to say. Maybe she didn't want to be. Not really.

The girls were silent now. That didn't take long. There was maybe some life left inside the flames, but even extinguished now, it would not carry long. They could not carry long. Both dead for . . . what? Being witches? Being the daughters of? Or, or, being in the eyesight of tragedy? Like the way star-stuff can sting, shaped into jagged bits that cut as they go down, slowly bleeding us out, whether under its water or not.

Like being crazy. Like being the brunt of the force. How perceived. After we burn ourselves down. And sure, maybe it wasn't exactly their selves what lit the flame, what bound their little hands round burned in

dreams wood. But it's all ourselves. Some just get
called witches so that there's a reason for the chaos in
our minds, in our lives, in our eyes.

I want to be,
mentally ill so,
i no, longer need to be
burned alive at the stake
for your simple mistakes
to notice when there's
sharp things on the table.
Like knife.
I want to be a knife.
So when I hold myself,
there's proof later.
Do you understand
me?
Cra see like maybe
gonna take my life
and kill my wife
with fire in children
accused of witchcraft
like emotions of
I'm irritated but can't tell you why.
So instead burn down the town.
Kill the hope pretended at in
clown grown from watered stone
in parks with purpose of death
and, breath like held water.
Hold me and feel the crazy in
trembling skin. Burn flesh.
Tragedy fresh.
Tragedy fresh.
In reverse movement to

explain
rain fallin' but skin dry,
eyes dry but heart cry,
and I see
that it's not my fault
not my fault
well, maybe . . .
Maybe dead under water
cause I talked you
into it.
Maybe, shouldn't sit
there alone when
there's friends to be made in
the woods of skins
we stopped cutting out loud.
And instead drowned
in front of their fathers.
Ma knew there was something to be had in front
of fathers. There was a dream like, have faith, in her
expression as she watched her children turn to smoke.
The cries were imagined. They were imagined
because, because the real thing was too hard to take.
It becomes too hard to take. In those times we, fake,
the things we think and feel, the things we think we
feel. The truth being too hollow. Too hollow to hold.
Have you ever felt your truth too hollow to hold? Did
you let it go? Did you make it heavier? Did you give it
to someone else? Made it another's truth. Truth in
blame. Remember the blame? The thing responsible
for two little girls being burned alive surrounded by a
crowd breathing them in. Scared of sickness. But
already let in. Let in and nurtured.

Nurtured the same as insecurities that grip onto

us as the sun goes down, and our love's not around, but maybe somewhere else, smelling a different scent, eating a different air, watching sunsets that don't quite match up. Was the truth of our things, whether hollow or not, that it never really matched up? Maybe enough could match to get along, to get by on most the time; but every so often, or sometimes damned so often, things would catch and we'd see that we are really just alone deciding whether or not to burn alive tonight, our own skin or someone else's. Someone else's.

The girls burned away to ash. Most didn't stay and watch the whole thing. Most quietly dragged their feet back to homes which now stood under what felt to be a permanent hue of orange happy flame. Only a few staying, late into the night, listening to the smoldering song as an ashy leg collapsed in here, an eye socket there. Even bone and teeth burned away under the heat of persecution. A different fire than, a campfire set for warmth and maybe something to eat. A fire that didn't provide but only took. Like the heat of the sun. But we haven't figured that out yet. That we are the energy given to the sun so it can burn alive in the universe. Maybe the first witch set to flame. Maybe the first daughter of witch. The human mythos like words on a page only able to see under the color of remember when.

She stayed out and listened to her children smoldering away all night and into daybreak of early morning. Had to. Was written somewhere on those same pages. A dense black soot covering her. The dense black soot of Francis. The dense black soot of Bel. Tear streaks down from eyes that looked so tired.

Nothing she could have done. Had she screamed at them that, YES! she was the witch; that YES! she had made their children sick? They'd of all been soot and ash collapsed in mounds gently smoking into the orange sky. Or maybe just her. Leaving the kids abandoned into the hands of savages like savages wearing masks under face paint. Better to be dead than abandoned. Even the pain of flames, thought Ma (Was she even still Ma?), paled in comparison to the pain of abandoned in this world. Alone in the seclusion of the American West. Alone in the seclusion of existing at all, maybe.

There was a metaphor somewhere in it. But she was too beaten down to figure what it was. Easy to feel that. Even without the fire eating us away. And after? Well in the after we must redefine. And we must do it quickly, before they come and take the rest from us.

CHAPTER 5
FUNERAL MARCH

PA COULD FEEL it in the breeze. There was death in the air in ways that wasn't so familiar as the hunger of nature devouring what it needed to keep going. And yet, maybe that was the universe at its core, devouring what it needed to keep going. Life the simultaneous creation and burning of energy to revolve something kin to what we can call existence. It all took energy, and it didn't care how it got what it needed. Like man. Not caring how it got what it needed. So long as it did, in fact, get what it needed. But what was that need? What was the need to exist? Was that a need at all? Any more than any other desire fabricating entire worlds so as to justify what it wanted to do? Fabrication of dream space for fear of the things we think in the dark when air is too thick for eyes to see through, and watch us touching at ourselves while we pretend we care about the cause and effect of skin that would catch fire if only we could let it. Let it catch fire for the elation of euphoria at how water splashes it back down, splashes flame to a quiet hush of smoke drifting off things we want but can't say for words that get too heavy when they are dirty. Pa felt it, not only in breeze of wind but in breeze of breath as he exhaled walking.

He'd headed back home. Again. After putting out memories of fires left behind. Again. It all feeling so familiar. It all always felt so familiar . . . didn't it? Doesn't it? Don't we live a life of footsteps we've already taken looking for things we know we ain't gonna find cause they wasn't there the first several thousand times we tried? Sure we do. Me. You. Pa. it didn't matter what we were called, or who were doing the calling. All been in the same place walking home, again, to new homes that smelled like old memories tied to stakes ready for burning once the smoke from before drifts high enough into the skies that we start truly believing they's somethin' we are supposed to call clouds. Mr. Cloud, in another life, thought Pa. Mr. Cloud in the same life only far enough away that the smell doesn't smell the same. He breathed in deeply. And in his breath he heard the screams he couldn't yet place but felt like they'd been meant for him in the dimensions traveled through on the way to the next. On the way to the next like tightrope death of gods getting too bored and lonely to take the darkness anymore. Was where we came in. In the darkness of distracting from. But distracting from what?

It was only early morning as Pa walked with that confident step he liked taking without noticing back into a town that he wanted so badly to pretend would be home. Something in him knew it wasn't, though. Maybe, really, everything, really . . . maybe everything in him knew it wasn't, knew it never was. All a pretend. And what was so bad about that? Nothing? Or, every-damned-thing? Tired of pretending that it meant something. Tired of finding new and the same ways in which to distract self from the inevitable occurrence of the tragic that lay ahead in quiet wait. Wait! The sky called down, screamed down, cried down to him but he refused to listen. Simply in too much hurry to get back to her, get back to the kids, and keep pretending.

He thought of the words he spoke to Bel as they first came to this place:

"'Pa, is there layers to the sky?' Jezebel's voice danced out in the heat like rain drops on leaf.

Her Pa stopped walking. Wiping the sweat simultaneously off his brow as he looked upwards into the sky, 'Reckon there's layers to everything,' turning to wink at her, 'don't you think so?'"

Like words out of a story book. Though this had been no story book. This had been a life lived in reverse, which acted like it moved forward. Try to remember what happens next, before it happens, and tell me that life had forward momentum. Life was something that came from rewinding rope used to hang heroes too caught up in roles to see that they were the villains the whole time. Was a funny thing, how that happened to the best of us. And how the worst of us envied it.

Would Pa be the villain, or the hero, he wondered, of his story, and laughed at the answer before question had full time to circle round his mind, gripping on tight like a snake preparing for dinner. And more importantly, did it really matter? Really make any type a difference?

Dusted road looked different under the rays of waking sun than stretching moon, Pa thought, or maybe something had changed. Was that it? Was life so very different now than it had been such a short time ago when he left to collect 'unfinished' business, like a ghost searching for old skin it once knew as home? Not life, in a general sense? But *his* life, in a specific sense? All we are, being the specific flavor of nightfall from the rest.

There was something outside their home as he neared. Something he couldn't quite make out as sun rose off in the distance, cascading its light on the scene same as fire rounding the corner in caves that used to keep us safe from things that flew in the night. But what kept us safe in our caves, in our homes, from us? Was there anything to protect us from our own reflection, our own shadow in the light of fires lit to illuminate the way? Nothing so powerful as of yet. Though perhaps there was still time left. Time left like time/space eating up the emptiness we thought was. Nothing like the drama of confusion to propel narrative. And as he neared even closer, a deep pit grew inside his stomach. This could not be. Not again. Not like this. When he thought he had found

just

enough

distance

from the past, here it was again to eat him alive, like so many times before, like so many lives before, like . . . like so many dies before.

Here it was. No knocking at the door but knocking at the soul like a hungry god back to collect what it lent us so we could live for a time and see, sort of, what it was like to exist. Such an awful, mean, trick. To giveth and taketh away in the same instant.

Though, could be that waiting too long only made it worse. Waiting too long only made it unbearable. And who could know that better than the Creator, in all His infinite glory. Well, if that was glory, we all must have thought simultaneously, the son-of-a-bitch could damn well keep it to Himself.

Feet hurried but didn't. Rushing past while standing still. As he came nearer and nearer the view he already knew what was. If he had lived this before . . . why must he live it again? But had he? Maybe all a dream. Maybe now a dream. 'Oh. My. Dear Lord. Please.' He spoke aloud in the infinite of space, 'please don't let it be true.' Though it was true. The pile of ash and tears told him more than he needed to know. This time there was no finding a new home. His had been burned down inside his daughters' skin.

The door creaked open. And she stood there, just inside, as though statue waiting for his return. She held what appeared to be baby James, not made of ash, in her arms which could have one day been as ash as the girls outside. One day if time were different. Or if time were the same. If time had been the same, same as it was before they intervened; well then how could one say she'd have not been ash, somewhere, somehow? There, as his great circle, even now. In truth, while Pa would never like to admit it, while we never do, our deepest truths are always the hardest to say, most never even having language that *can* speak them; especially now, his great circle. 'What the fuck happened?'

There was accusatory in his voice. Accusatory that she didn't know just how to deal with, how to process. It all meant the same. Sure. But not his. Not from him. From him it was something different that stung more in the look steaming away from him like breath in cold winter's wind. All our meaning like that, breathed away in the chill of air laughing at us as we simply try to survive. If he'd have asked "are you okay" . . . She would have had the space to lie and say no. We're always okay. Have to be. No other choice. If existing then we were "okay."

'All I want,' her voice began, wanting to pretend at strength but not having the stability, 'is a little time to not be okay. A little time to be broken.'

'Somethin' tells me you'll have plenty!'

But she wouldn't. No no. She'd have something quite like the opposite. With death having breathed its hot fiery breath on her door, flames nearly forced down her throat, she'd have to be more okay than ever before. 'What would you know about it, anyway?'

'What's there left to mourn with, huh?! Tell me. What have you left us?'

'I?! I have left nothing. It was all taken from me!' There was a silence in the air as things decided what direction they tended to head in. Things analyzing their own trajectory to see where the two headed. Like always as we decide what to say next. Or, pretend to decide, in any case, as there's so much involved who's to say it's us what does the deciding. 'I have you,' her eyes softened at him, 'us. We have him,' she lifted James up so gently as he slept in her arms. Peace offering as the scent of their burned children still flowed in the breeze surrounding them. 'There was nothing I could do. They came. They came in the night and *you* weren't here. Were you?' Eyes searching the darkness along the floor.

'They had it in their heads that . . . that Bel, that Francis, was the cause of their sickness.'

'In their heads that Bel and Francis . . . or that *you* was the cause?'

'Say what you mean.'

'You coward. They came for you and you gave 'em them. Didn't you?' And again, more forcefully but not, 'Didn't you!'

'What was I to do? Abandon them all to whatever cruelty this world has in store? Abandon them? Abandon you? Death is better.'

His tears burned down face. They ached with tiredness an' old age. They ached from the same, over and over. The same sort of maintenance as the pains we live. Part of him not wanting them to flow in front of her. Part of him knowing there was no point in trying to control anything else in the scene. Part of him just wanting to hold her. 'Death is better?' He mumbled out. 'Death is better.'

Death was the great abandoner. And it had come to them so often. It comes to all of us so often. In every day's breath under the freshly painted sun in the sky. We are dying. They say how tomorrow is a brand new day. But under the glaring eye of death. Brand new means little. Brand new meant an existence we no longer connect to. And it left us . . . it left us abandoned, in the darkness of all alone. Though she stood there. And now so too did he. And they weren't alone. They weren't alone for a brief time, but knew that it would not last long. *That* being almost worse than anything else. The foreknowledge that connection was only a drifting distant memory dancing in used-to-be times of I was once not so lonely. Smoke burned that away. Sure, they said it weren't the smoke what done the burning but the flames. But there was some intent in smoke like left-over that seemed to suggest something different in the process.

'I just wanted to stop burning. I thought you wanted the same too.'

'I did. I . . . I do. Maybe that pushed it on us even more.'

'Don't you feel that loneliness? Don't you feel it like we've been here before? And at who's will? At yours? At mine? At . . . At theirs? Was it their will to be burned alive?'

'Still looking at a reason behind all this. Like there is one. Like if'in there were, it'd be something you'd wanna look at. Ever think that? Ever think that maybe we can't see the reasons because what they'd mean to us?'

'I'm just tired of the hurting. Of living off it like it's fuckin' air, like it's . . . water. Water. That's what it was wasn't it. The water got to 'em. And Jezebel wasn't scared. And . . . And that was enough wasn't it? To set the ball rolling like moss growing on grave. We really are a fungus aren't we. We're a mold that eats away at our own sanity for nourishment. Hunger to death eventually. Then start in on the rest. No reality left once we've had our fill. All eaten. Isn't that it? All eaten.'

And he watched her. For movement.

And she knew what he was going to do.

But she pretended not to. Pretended because, maybe, maybe this time it would mean something to the outcome. Maybe this time things would be different.

'I'll do what you were too scared to. It's not too late.'

'Please don't.' As he turned and walked out of their pretense at home.

'It's not too late.'

It was. It was too late and they both knew it. Knew it so that 'too late' didn't even really make any sense. Too late implied there was a moment when it could have been differently, and that that moment had passed, and that here we were, or are. It was only ever headed in the one direction, though. All of it was all headed in the only direction it could be. That was the way things were. It's the way things are. Pa's steps out into the dirt were preordained since the first of moments, whenever and wherever that did come from. God, he hoped, if asked, but he wasn't sure why? Exactly. For what else he tried to believe in the world. In this world. Our world. Getting in the way. The way of God. The way of others.

He could feel it as he moved. That she knew this was coming. His words tended to linger somewhere for now, leaving him only with a loud guttural cry to howl out into the air filling up the town, 'AAAAHHHHhhhhhrrrRRR!' Bursting inside all the air. In every breath of sleeping beauty, and monster, and everything in between. If there were an in between. For so long many claiming that's where truth was, where things met and evened out. Though more and more it seemed, to those like Pa, that it was in the farthest ends that we found truth. The edges of officious orbits organizing orgies painted presumptuously in black and white. Black of the earth. White of the sky. Horizon being indifferent to existence. And what good was that?

'AAAAHHHHhhhhhrrrRRR!' Pa called out again like an animal. No. Not like. But as an animal. The calls of animals in pain. The hurt in us. Like the hurt in us all. Every bit floating into the universe, collected up in one call. And the townsfolk felt it. They all knew it was them. Them in the guts of others. And they cried. Whether sitting in fire lit night, or sleeping restlessly through blazing dreams. Tears fell from eyes and rolled like stones down mountains. Picking up momentum through and through. Tumbling down for the tragedies that you felt in your life. Us all, having them. We being Pa. Or any other, for that matter. Something in the pain knew it as well. And it grew; grew a lifetime in that instant of the set-in of wounded animal calling for . . . for . . . for someone to make it all stop.

Making it stop in the ways that knew, the process that knew, there was no real stop to it. But they came anyway. They slumped out of bed, rubbing at teary eyes weary from nightmare sleep. They stumbled from chairs soaked with the sweat of what had yet to come. They came anyway.

Pa imagined, as they came out into the street like slow statues, that they had grown into some sort of creature. Sprouting from the tops of their nightshirts and coats, instead of neck and head, a green type of moss-covered stub. Features shadowed onto the surface like tales of mystery. Something that was at one time face, but now, now only the memory of what nature thought it looked like. They stood around, near enough, 'I!' Pa yelled out when words could be formed, 'I am the one . . . I am responsible for all your loss!' Used-to-be faces looking around at each other. Taking in their shadows? Seeing them as faces? They murmured gasps of not shock but something like, something that wanted to be. 'I am the witch you seek. The demon you hunt out of children is standing here before you! What will you do now? With your poisoned spite? With your judgement?!'

They closed in tighter around him. Their murmurs turned from confused to gleeful. This had been the closure they sought. Something so, unsatisfying about the way the girls' burned bodies broke away as ash crumbled into coals. This had been it. It was their father responsible for the pains they had had to endure, would have to endure. Some felt guilt at burning the girls alive, needlessly. Others knew that Pa had deserved that taste of their sorrow before his own judgement. Their beady green shadows watching him to soak up every bit of the sadness drenching off his body like waterfall shook from fur.

'Do what you will.' His words careless in their delivery. 'Do what you must.' And broke apart. He could feel his great circle watching from just outside their doorway. He missed the way she now looked at him. And maybe that was what this had all been about. It was drama to recreate spaces taken away by time moving to and to and further and further away from anything he could pretend to have known and into moments that looked like the life lived before but only in a foreign-not-quite-real but wants to be so very badly type of way. A drama to make her need to look at him. Need like that. Need at all. He knew they would hang him before they announced in unison, 'Hang the witch!' like carolers singing out the praise of the Lord. He knew they'd disperse, back to their homes, except for the few who'd head to build the gallows intended for the hanging. And they did. Wandering away, knowing that Pa needed the hanging as much as they needed to do it, so no reason to tie him down or drag him off now, not till the wood had been nailed, least. Leaving them standing in the dirt alone. Not quite day. Not quite night. But some orange hue of a universe that would never exactly step out of the shadow again.

She imagined this space so very many times. The inevitable story line that was coming, looming, like brightly lit clouds hovering in some version of existence that looked exactly like the one we chose to live through. There was nothing unusual about it. There was nothing *maybe* about it. Nothing whatsoever. It had been coming same as any other moment. They only being able to put it off for so long. Acting like, even to some degree, they had been here before, had lived this before, and so would live again, and maybe, well, who knew . . . (?) . . . change it somehow that time around. Tease oneself into belief that the inevitable had been lived out, and was over and done with. But was it? Or was it just building up to come back round for another turn at blood and tears and ashes and bones and burnins and yearnins and hangings and . . . and she'd miss him if that was the case. Miss them, too. Miss through a universe that, when all was said and done, really only seemed designed for that one purpose. All built up so we could fall away, crumble away, rebuilding just to break apart again.

Yeah. She'd miss him alright. Like childhood memories. Like crisp lemonade smell on tongue. Like sweet kiss on lips. Like love. Like children. Like . . . children. But no use in thinking that. No use in thinking on what had to be. What of it had to be? And what of it chose to be? Didn't matter. They were there. They were there and so had to do . . . something, right? Had to do something.

'We have to do something.' She whispered off far enough that she thought he wouldn't even hear the words, but taste their remnants.

'We are doing something. Dying for the sins we couldn't wash off.' Wash off like rainwater washing wounds left open to heal. By creatures that knew that wasn't how things worked. By things laughing at the fester growing in us till faces were only shadows and souls couldn't see anymore.

It took the better part of a day for it to be constructed. Which, for the gravitas of the moment it existed for, would seem ever so short an amount of time. Folks never seeming to take the time in the spaces where time is needed most. Though could be any time, suppose, that needed the time the most. And no time to give. To have. Being ready the following morning. Pa was, somehow, disappointed in the distortion of the hue of the day. In how risen the sun indeed felt. Always contradictions, he thought, while still standing outside waiting. He didn't move much from that spot, the spot he stood in as the creatures who'd used to be townsfolk, wandered off back to their homes, or back to build gallows, the day before. No reason. Was only waiting. Static in life like so many before had advised against.

Static brought death, they'd say. Children pretending to be adults with wisdom to sell, though to get you hooked they'd give away the first bits for free.

Once hooked. Well then the words took over thoughts and there was no escape. Stuck payin' to be alive. Always some price to pay, reckon, and so did Pa. And so, he stayed, and waited for what was left to come. Feeling like the days we were alive; stuck waitin' on what was left to come. What was left to come? After the children died? After we left each other alone to take care of takin' care of? The universe, no, the existence *of* the universe never happy with its fill. Glutton for *our* punishment through holes in its fabric eaten by worms. Too cowardly to go through it itself. It sends others. And hopes to gain . . . (?) . . . insight into self through the reports, or bits of screamed data, as we burn alive? All we were was information collected as we cried alone at night in agony of death. Agony of life forced. Which was, abandon in the dark; what had she said; worse than death. It was all worse than death. All worse than; it was why Pa didn't bother moving, and only waited, still, er, fairly still, till he heard that trumpet blare sounding the ready.

We are all sounding the ready as we hyperventilate in panic attack mind.

Confined to, panic attack finding us inside guts called memory.

Member me, when the skin falls off and the pain starts to show.

Remember me when we both feel so low

that we'd rather stay than go even when the flames burn, slow

slow, so slow to start, but remember, play the part, and so they

find a bit enough time to make our thoughts tremble down spine

because mine

was left out in the rain too long, fear of drowning in

self like the songs of our own death frowning in;

do you remember what it's like to kill yourself?

I remember what it's like to want to be, left alone with you.

All memory that memory could have if tried.

Died like drowning each other before the

others get to us first, with a thirst for,

making us pay for the things they couldn't find in life.

Wife and kids and meaning and bleeding and seeding and seed me and

Won't you grow me like no one's watching, even as they pry in?

I want you to begin, for them, but let them, think, they finished.

Can you do that for me? See I can't stop the breathing, that stops my breathing

without you letting me end the way I, need, be, I

need to be what you fantasized about before faces lost eyes

and skin grew green like things unseen in the slimy deeps

of oceans taunting children to climb in.

Climb in as I hang here. And tell me how to restart.

Climb in. Before we part.

She would climb in. And come with him. Of course. Of course, they both knew it as feet began again. Our stories told in our footsteps. Was why they came round so often; to carry us through to the next point in the plot.

Pa wanted it to mean more. He could hear her behind, next, to him as they walked towards the end. In all honesty he had imagined this moment so very many times. And they, each and every one of them, imagined deaths, carried with them so much more blatantly than it seemed now, as they were in it. But that was probably many things; so much more than when we are in it. Or maybe this was just a poor imagining. Maybe he was still standing, waiting. Or he was sleeping on the trail back home and only dreaming this drama. Did he want that? He wondered. Would that he could? Was this just the time? God damn always just the time.

The town ebbed out into desert in such a way he hadn't remembered before that made him question maybe he didn't know where he was. Eyes squinting in the desert heat, the desert sand dusted into hotter than moments before air. His skin felt rough as though lived in such a place since eyes opened into a world that could not be remembered. This could not be remembered. Pa turned slightly to look at her. She had been crying but wouldn't show him. Hiding the tears like witches hiding children. Big round eyes like big round ovens.

Hiding for what? Hiding for him? That's what she meant. But it wasn't the truth. The truth was something else entirely. Something else that didn't matter much here. Laughter wanting at bursting through lips. Now was likely not the time. When did truth ever matter, really? And he let out a tamed guffaw.

'Laughter?' She questioned. Though neither had spoken a word. Laughter in dying times. Could we respond. Though at a point we can't. At a point it's . . . It's . . . It's all too fucking much. Was that what we were meant for? At the end of all this? All too much? The only space we, time and time again come back to? It was meant for excess? *We* were meant for excess? 'Our biggest sin is excess?' He questioned. Though neither had said a word. Her dress blew in the dry breeze. 'I missed you while you were gone.' Words, honest. 'I know.' Honesty only goes so far. 'I'm sorry I went back.' She smiled at him, 'I just . . . It doesn't go away, you know?' She did. 'I know. I forgive you, Thomas. I shouldn't even have to say it.' 'I mostly just like hearin' you say it. Is all.' She watched him tightly. Not sure what feelings. 'I know.' And they both smiled as their bodies shuddered at the things they tried to control. 'I have to do this. You know that.' 'It's already done, darling, we *both* know that.' Didn't want to but did. So many of the spaces any of us are in. Didn't want to but did. The suffering we go through. Watching our children grow up. Watching everything drift, slowly away, from what we know and into fear of waking till one day, drift so far, that one day eyes just don't open any more. That day is now. Here. For Tom. The girls. My God. The girls. He thought. Letting a shudder work its way and drop tear after tear after tear from now felt as though had never been dry eyes. They couldn't have deserved his failures. Could they? Could she? Thoughts swirling in chaotic brain. What did happen down there by the water? So many years ago? What was it that kept following them no matter where they went? What is it that follows us around as we die pretending to live and keeps us so fucking sad? It's all too much. And he watched the stairs leading up. It's all too much. And he could feel the noose round his neck.

'I don't remember, what I did to deserve this life. But it must have been me. It must have been so deeply rooted as to never let go. And I'm sorry. Though that doesn't seem to matter much.'

The beginning fades, as we try to remember it. Knowing, this may not be the end, but it's far enough away that surely the beginning must be dead. Hard to watch beginnings die. But we do it all the time. Harder yet, to watch 'em through the smoke of loved ones who paid the price for our own tendencies. But we do it all the time. In truth, see, that priceless petulant pedantic particle; we all were the witches responsible for not just the craft in the world, but also, maybe, the effects of those. Cause and effect of the existing. And the ash we breathe it through. A dying memory of sacrifice, sacrifice that Pa had made far too many times to count. And would a time or two more.

THEY BUILT A GALLOWS FOR YOU
AND ME
(POSTHUMOUS EDITION)

DUST SWARMED AND created a veil between the two lovers.
Eyes crusted oceans.
Hand hesitant in the air,
confused by old habits in movement.
Emptiness. For miles and miles.
She could taste his tears, 'You don't have to.
We can just go.'
He flinched.
'I can't see you,' wind calming on cue,
sand falling gently on shoulders,
in hair, finding home back on the ground,
'through all this.'
'That's why we're here,' he mumbled out as knuckles
half-heartedly rapped against the clean,
bright smelling wood of the gallows.
'It's hard to hear you when . . . '
'YEAH IT'S FUCKING HARD TO HEAR ME ISN'T IT!?' Skin painted red from the inside out, 'that's why we're here.'

She clenched her jaw.
Wishing he would, like he used to.
Anything to see
him hurting again. Knowing her fingertips
on his warm skin would sooth him,
razor blades hungrily eating through soft flesh.
Blood drip drip dripping onto tiled floor like
faucets with blown O-rings.
She knew how to clean that mess up.
'Nothing's going to fix it. Except a tight rope and
a quick drop.'
'I can take the baby and go. I'm sorry. You can
start fresh.'
'I didn't want to start fresh,' voice a broken record,
'I wanted you . . . I wanted . . . '
An automaton inside living skin.
Cold hands reaching for tightly wound rope.
And as he slowly pulled the noose round his
anxious neck,
something changed in the landscape.
Figures rose out of the dirt. Crumbling
bits here and there,
crashing to the ground, clumps of dirt exploding
with loud busts like birds blown apart with
firecrackers.
What could she do but watch his performance
now?
Listen for the break of his bones?
Breathing, heavy and patterned with sadness.
She whispered through closed lips, 'I love you,'
like she used to. So long ago when he could still
see her thoughts in her eyes. But now . . . now he
didn't notice.

Quickly pulled the lever.
And suddenly,
violently,
he slammed into the ground.
Rope snapped screaming old apologies for its failure.
Dirt pretending at executioner audience
fell apart and blew into the wind.
He breathed in deeply, mouthfuls of ground, sky, sun.
He could taste her through the dry earth,
a gentle breeze through summer picnic memories.
And she sobbed.
Hands reached to throat as though twins separated
by hundreds of miles who still somehow mimicked each other's actions.
She wanted to rush over to him.
It was surely a sign that God, or the universe,
or whatever wanted him to live through this space.
But she didn't.
She knew he already heard the whispers in the hot desert heat.
Already had a plan to get through it.
A plan that involved razor blades,
and shadows,
and stitching darkness into blood.
A plan to hang through the memories of ash.